THERE WAS ONLY ONE WAY TO PROPERLY ANSWER SIR JUSTIN'S SHOCKING PROPOSAL

When Margaret heard that Sir Justin Keighley had demanded her in marriage, her reaction was instant. She set out on foot to run away from home and find a new and independent life.

Alas, it was in vain. Sir Justin finally caught up with her. And here on the deserted highway, he clearly was determined to make her return with him. By force if necessary.

Fortunately, Margaret was prepared to answer him. From her sachel she drew the loaded pistol she'd had the good sense to pack.

"Where did you get that?" said Sir Justin. "Put it away and stop being ridiculous."

A moment later, Sir Justin was lying on the ground, a red stain spreading on his shoulder.

That, of course, should have been the end of everything between them. Instead it was just the beginning—and a mere nothing compared to what was to come. . . .

A RADICAL ARRANGEMENT

SIGNET Regency Romances You'll Want to Read

(0451)

- [ ] **THE MAKESHIFT MARRIAGE by Sandra Heath.**
  (122682—$2.25)*
- [ ] **FASHION'S LADY by Sandra Heath.** (118294—$2.25)*
- [ ] **MALLY by Sandra Heath.** (093429—$1.75)*
- [ ] **MANNERBY'S LADY by Sandra Heath.** (097726—$1.95)*
- [ ] **THE OPERA DANCER by Sandra Heath.** (111125—$2.25)*
- [ ] **THE SHERBORNE SAPPHIRES by Sandra Heath.**
  (115139—$2.25)*
- [ ] **THE UNWILLING HEIRESS by Sandra Heath.**
  (097718—$1.95)*
- [ ] **THE HEADSTRONG WARD by Jane Ashford.** (122674—$2.25)*
- [ ] **THE MARCHINGTON SCANDAL by Jane Ashford.**
  (116232—$2.25)*
- [ ] **THE THREE GRACES by Jane Ashford.** (114183—$2.25)*
- [ ] **THE CLERGYMAN'S DAUGHTER by Julia Jefferies.**
  (120094—$2.25)*
- [ ] **THE CHADWICK RING by Julia Jefferies.** (113462—$2.25)*

*Prices slightly higher in Canada.

Buy them at your local bookstore or use this convenient coupon for ordering.

THE NEW AMERICAN LIBRARY, INC.,
P.O. Box 999, Bergenfield, New Jersey 07621

Please send me the books I have checked above. I am enclosing $_____
(please add $1.00 to this order to cover postage and handling). Send check
or money order—no cash or C.O.D.'s. Prices and numbers are subject to change
without notice.

Name_____

Address_____

City _____ State _____ Zip Code _____
Allow 4-6 weeks for delivery.
This offer is subject to withdrawal without notice.

A
Radical
Arrangement

by
Jane Ashford

A SIGNET BOOK
NEW AMERICAN LIBRARY
TIMES MIRROR

SIGNET TRADEMARK REG. U.S. PAT. OFF. AND FOREIGN COUNTRIES
REGISTERED TRADEMARK—MARCA REGISTRADA
HECHO EN CHICAGO, U.S.A.

SIGNET, SIGNET CLASSIC, MENTOR, PLUME, MERIDIAN AND NAL BOOKS
are published by The New American Library, Inc.,
1633 Broadway, New York, New York 10019

First Printing, October, 1983

1 2 3 4 5 6 7 8 9

PRINTED IN THE UNITED STATES OF AMERICA

1

"Now, Margaret," said Mrs. Mayfield, leaning forward to adjust one of her iron-gray curls before her dressing-table mirror, "you must remember that the party invited for dinner tonight is a rather unusual one."

"Yes, Mama," replied the thin, pale girl standing behind her chair.

"Your father's position as Member of Parliament for the district requires him to receive a number of people who are not quite, er, our sort. And when we come down here to Devon in the summer months, he must see all the major landholders, whether they support him or not. Now that you are out, you will be joining these gatherings."

"Yes, Mama."

Mrs. Mayfield eyed her reflection critically, turning her head to observe the new lace cap she had set upon it. "Tonight," she continued, "we will have Sir Justin Keighley. His estate is the largest in the neighborhood, and we cannot afford to ignore him, much as we should like to. I believe I have mentioned him to you before."

Margaret nodded, her large blue eyes widening even farther. She had received a great many instructions from her mother before her debut in London last season, but none had been so explicit or vehement as the warning against their neighbor Justin Keighley.

"The man is thoroughly unsound," added her mother with a certain relish.

"Not only is he a gambler and a libertine, his political views are shocking. He is more radical than Lord Holland. You will scarcely credit it, Margaret, but he has expressed sympathy for those Yorkshiremen who smashed a factoryful of power looms last month."

Margaret drew in her breath. She had been very strictly reared in a religious family, but no sin she knew of was worse than this. In the conservative Tory circles her parents illuminated, the merest hint of radicalism caused shudders and references to France under Robespierre. Sir Justin Keighley was not far removed from the devil himself in Margaret Mayfield's mind.

"You will, of course, keep out of his way," finished her mother, rising and shaking out the folds of her lavender silk evening dress. "I simply wished to alert you to his presence. I daresay it won't signify, with Philip here." She smiled benignly, without really altering her rather harsh-featured face. Margaret had fulfilled all her parents' expectations by becoming engaged in her first season, at nineteen, to the very eligible, and eminently sound, Philip Manningham. Their families had been acquainted for years and had similar habits and interests. Margaret had received Philip's addresses without surprise, and he had taken her acceptance as a matter of course. To all observers the couple seemed as satisfied as their elders with the arrangement. Margaret, a belated and solitary offspring of two strong-willed people, brought the promise of a large inheritance and her father's political connections to the match. Philip possessed an equal fortune and even larger ambitions. And he found Margaret's well-schooled timidity exactly to his taste.

"Let me look at you," commanded Mrs. Mayfield,

turning from the mirror to survey her daugher. "That gown is pretty. You always look sweet in white." She examined Margaret's very pale blond hair, dressed in languid ringlets about her head, the modest single strand of pearls encircling her thin neck, and her white satin evening dress. "Your waist is hanging loose again," she commented sharply. "Have you been eating properly, Margaret? How many times do I have to tell you that you are too thin?"

The girl hung her head. "I do *try*, Mama. But I am never very hungry."

"Nonsense." Mrs. Mayfield cast a complacent glance over her own well-padded figure. "You picked at your luncheon in the most annoying way. You do *not* make the least effort. You must do better at dinner tonight. And try to show a little animation."

Margaret swallowed nervously. "Yes, Mama."

"We may as well go down. Our guests will be arriving in half an hour. Don't forget what I've told you."

"No, Mama."

Mrs. Mayfield looked up sharply, half annoyed at her daughter's listless tone, half suspecting irony. But Margaret was gazing vacantly at the carpet: her pale cheeks showed no hint of guilt or excitement. Mrs. Mayfield shook her head. Her only child had been a model of obedience and propriety since her earliest years; it was only her mother's exposure to a very different sort of girl in London, an exposure that had left Mrs. Mayfield reeling with scandalized outrage, that had awakened such ridiculous suspicions in her breast. Margaret had never, and never would, exhibit anything but gentle acquiescence. It was a measure, thought her mother, of her own and her husband's sound principles.

Ralph Mayfield and Philip Manningham were already in the drawing room when the ladies entered. They stood on opposite sides of the fireplace, engaged, as usual, in political debate. Though they agreed on every important point, they never tired of rehearsing their opinions and reviling their opponents'. Mrs. Mayfield moved eagerly to join them, but Margaret drifted over to one of the long windows and gazed out at the garden. The July twilight still lingered, and she could see the military rows of her mother's roses stretching to the wall. She sighed softly, but none of the others noticed.

The first of the guests to arrive was the local squire, Henry Camden, with his wife and daughter. The Mayfields greeted them cordially, and the talk shifted from politics to farming without a pause. Mrs. Camden was as absorbed as her husband in this topic, and at least two of her hosts were astute enough to appear interested. Alice Camden, the squire's eighteen-year-old daughter, came to sit beside Margaret. "I have not yet wished you happy," she began. "We saw the announcement of your engagement in the *Morning Post*."

"Thank you," replied Margaret.

"When is the wedding to be?"

"I'm not certain. Mama thinks perhaps in the autumn."

Miss Camden stared. She and Margaret were not particularly well acquainted. Though they had grown up within two miles of each other and were nearly of an age, Margaret's mother had always kept her close and Alice had been more than satisfied with her own sisters and brothers as playmates. But they did know each other, and Alice could see no reason for the other girl's lack of enthusiasm about her wedding date. In Miss Camden's view, the question ought to arouse intense emotion in any young woman so blessed.

Margaret, gazing at the Turkey carpet, did not notice her frown, however. And the entrance of two more dinner guests effectively ended their exchange.

The new arrivals were John and Maria Twitchel, important residents of the nearby market town. He was a solicitor and she the daughter of a Devon clergyman, and both were very conscious of the solemnity of the occasion— their annual dinner at the Mayfield house. Mr. Twitchel at once shifted the conversation back to politics, local this time, and the possibility of an election in the coming year. The Mayfields and Philip Manningham responded passionately, feebly seconded by the squire, leaving Mrs. Twitchel to the other women. The talk had grown somewhat heated, and the volume a bit loud, when the butler announced the final guest in a penetrating tone. As one, the group fell silent and turned.

Sir Justin Keighley stood in the doorway, looking them over with a slight, satirical curve of his lips. He wore, like the other gentlemen, conventional evening dress, but this superficial similarity was their only common ground. Ralph Mayfield, Philip Manningham, the squire, and John Twitchel were none of them unattractive men or negligible personalities. Each, in his own sphere, had a certain dignity and authority, and all had the confidence that respect engendered. Yet somehow, the moment he entered the room and before he spoke a word, Justin Keighley eclipsed them. It was not charm. Indeed, the newcomer did not look at all pleasant or ingratiating. And it was not mere social position. Keighley held an ancient baronetcy and a substantial fortune, but any of twenty men his hosts were accustomed to meeting ranked above him. Ralph Mayfield could not have said why he felt subdued as he came forward to greet his final guest.

The squire's wife might have enlightened him. As she had told a friend at a Bath assembly two years ago, "Justin Keighley is a vastly attractive man, my dear. And not just to women. All the young men ape him, my son among them. I don't know just how it is, but he has a great influence without appearing to seek it in the least. Indeed, sometimes I think he dislikes the idea. But it

goes on. It's something in his manner. No doubt you've
noticed it yourself. He *makes* you look at him." Mrs.
Camden had been embarrassed by this speech, but it was
quite true. And Keighley's attraction was the more myste-
rious because he was not conventionally handsome. Though
tall and well made, with broad shoulders and a good leg,
his features were rough—a jutting nose and heavy black
brows that nearly obscured expressive hazel eyes. And he
took no care with his dress, a rarity in an elegant age.
His coats were made so that he could shrug himself into
them without help; his collars did not even approach his
jaw; and he had once been observed in White's with a
distinct thumb mark on his Hessian boots, giving one of
the dandy set what he described as "a shuddering
palpitation."

But these sartorial eccentricities were outweighed by
Sir Justin's political influence and sagacity. He was an
intimate of the Prince Regent and Lord Holland, and
important in the Whig Party. These facts did not explain
his fascination for a great number of people, chiefly
women, who hadn't the slightest interest in politics, but
they amply justified the Mayfields' attention and suppressed antipathy

"Good evening," Keighley said to Mr. Mayfield in a
deep, resonant voice. "I hope I haven't kept you waiting."

"Not at all, not at all. Come in. You know everyone, I
think."

Sir Justin bowed his head with a sardonic smile. He
always met precisely the same people at his yearly dinner
with the Mayfields, presumably those they were certain
he could not "corrupt" with his aberrant opinions, and he
always felt the same infuriated boredom. For the fiftieth
time he wondered why he came. There was no hope of
amusement or chance of advantage here. The Mayfields
and their friends were just the sort of smug, resolutely
conventional people he despised. They held to the views

their fathers had bequeathed them and attacked all others. If one tried to make them change even a fraction, they shook their heads and muttered of treason.

He looked around the room. The only addition this year was the Mayfields' daughter. He had forgotten her name, but he remembered that she had come out last season. She looked as one would have expected: a pallid, simpering creature. Keighley shrugged. Politics forced him to endure fools occasionally. The Prince would want to know the climate of opinion here in Devon. He supposed he could get through this evening as he had previous ones, through a combination of stoicism and bitter inner laughter.

Magaret watched him with awed apprehension as he settled beside Mrs. Camden and began to chat with her about London. She had never actually spoken to Sir Justin; her mother had seen to that. But she had heard him talked of so many times that she felt she knew what he would say in response to a wide variety of remarks. It would always be shocking. She gazed at him in an effort to understand how any man could be so utterly depraved in thought and action, almost expecting his rugged face to contort in a grimace of malevolence and his chiseled lips to emit some horrifying revelation.

Suddenly Sir Justin looked up and met her eyes from across the room. He seemed at first startled to find her staring, then his mocking smile appeared again, and he raised one black brow, holding her gaze. Embarrassed, Margaret tried to look away, but something in his hazel eyes prevented it. A spark glinted there, and she felt a kind of tremor along her nerves. It was utterly unfamiliar and unsettling, like a violent thrill of feeling. How could a stranger affect her so? This must be fear, she thought; I am afraid of him. She began to tremble, but still she could not turn her head away. He seemed to understand her reaction and, amused, to prolong the contact on purpose.

Finally Keighley laughed and bent to answer some question of Mrs. Camden's. Margaret jerked back in her chair and clasped her shaking hands so tightly that the knuckles whitened. He was a dreadful man. She would not speak to him, and if she ever saw him again, she would run away.

Dinner was announced a few minutes later, and the party went into the dining room. Margaret, safely seated between the squire and Mr. Twitchel, each of whom found his opposite partner more engrossing, was free to toy with the food on her plate and try to recover her composure. This was made difficult by the fact that Sir Justin was almost opposite, but he did not look at her again. Indeed, he spent most of the meal flirting with Alice Camden, whom Mrs. Mayfield had ruthlessly sacrificed to a man she had more than once stigmatized as "unfit to speak to young girls." But as she had told her husband the previous day, one of the girls must sit beside him, and it was not going to be Margaret.

They had reached the dessert course without mishap when the squire, who had partaken rather too freely of Mr. Mayfield's excellent claret, leaned forward and addressed his host down the length of the table. "I say, Mayfield, I understand you have a very promising heifer in this season's group. Championship lines, eh?"

Mrs. Mayfield frowned at this breach of dinner-table etiquette, but her husband could not restrain a complacent smile. "Indeed, yes," he replied. "A fine animal. My cowman is extremely pleased."

"I'd like to see her."

"Certainly. Come round any day and I'll—"

"Leaving for m'sister's place tomorrow morning," interrupted the squire, clearly feeling the effects of the wine.

"Ah," responded his host. "Too bad."

"What say we see her tonight? Daresay the whole company would enjoy it."

Mrs. Mayfield looked stunned. The squire's wife said, "Now, Henry," and his daughter's lower lip trembled. The Twitchels' faces froze in the look that respectable people assume when one of their number begins to make a fool of himself. Margaret hunched in her chair and stared at her plate.

"What a splendid idea," drawled Sir Justin Keighley, drawing the astonished gaze of every other diner. His own hazel eyes were twinkling, and he obviously enjoyed their response as much as the squire's suggestion. "I should like to see this exceptional animal."

"Told you so," said the squire owlishly. "Everyone would." Doubt seemed to shake him for a moment. "That is, perhaps the ladies—"

"*I* shall certainly come," interrupted his wife, clearly determined to ride herd on Camden.

He merely grinned at her. "Course you will. Always pluck up to the backbone."

"And I'm sure Miss Camden will wish to join us," added Keighley smoothly, smiling at the girl.

"I . . ." Alice Camden looked as if it were the last thing she wanted, but she hadn't the social address to demur politely.

Mrs. Mayfield was another matter. "*Nonsense*," she said. "It is pitch dark. We cannot go to the barns at this time of night in our evening dress. Anyone who wishes to see the, er, cow can come back another day."

"There is a full moon," answered Sir Justin. "It is quite light outside." Mrs. Mayfield glared at him with the full strength of her formidable temper, but he merely continued to smile.

"Full moon," echoed the squire, nodding. He pushed himself unsteadily to his feet. "Let's go, then."

Keighley also rose, offering his arm to Alice Camden with a quizzical look. She, after one helpless, appealing glance at her mother, stood and took it.

"Very well," said Mrs. Mayfield through clenched teeth. "We shall *all* go and look at the wretched creature." And, pushing her chair back abruptly, she swept out into the hall. The rest of the party followed with varying degrees of uneasiness.

At the back door, their hostess met them with cloaks for the ladies. She did not speak again as they put them on and, one by one, stepped out into the mild July night. There was indeed a full moon, and it shed a surprising amount of silvery light, though the group also took three lanterns. Mr. Mayfield led the party through the garden and onto a gravel drive that led to the outbuildings. The Squire strode happily along beside him, chatting about cattle breeding and seemingly oblivious to the violent emotions he had aroused in more than one of the females behind them.

Margaret gradually dropped behind the others. She disliked cows and didn't at all want to walk through the barns in her white satin gown. But neither did she want to attract any of her mother's barely suppressed bad temper to herself by saying anything. She thought perhaps if she slipped away quietly and waited somewhere outside, she could rejoin the others later without comment. Had she dared, she would have returned to the house, but this seemed too much to venture.

The group was walking rapidly, and in a few moments Margaret was alone on the gravel path, listening to their voices drift off ahead. She stopped and looked around for a bench she knew to be nearby. She would wait here for their return. But even as she saw it and started forward a movement caught her eye, and Sir Justin Keighley materialized out of the darkness to stand before her. "I saw you drop back," he said, "and I suddenly found I hadn't the slightest wish to see this fabulous cow."

Margaret had started violently at his appearance. Now she began to tremble as she had earlier under his magnetic gaze. How could she escape? He stood between her and the safety of the group.

Keighley's eyes twinkled, though his face remained impassive. A more experienced observer than Margaret might have suspected he was teasing her. "Has your garden other points of interest?" he asked. "Perhaps we could indulge in a moonlight stroll while the others are in the barns." He raised one black brow and offered his arm. Margaret swallowed and tried to speak, but no words came out. She had never imagined in her worst nightmares that she would be left alone with the man her mother had characterized as "immoral, impious, and thoroughly untrustworthy." One side of Keighley's mouth jerked. "Surely there must be something worth seeing?" he added. "An ornamental pond in the moonlight? An avenue of limes? No? I can scarcely credit it. Let us explore and see what we can find." He took Margaret's hand and pulled her arm through his, causing her to tremble even more violently.

"I c-can't," the girl finally managed. "I must g-go to Mama."

"Oh, they will be along in a moment," answered Sir Justin. "They cannot linger long over a heifer. We will no doubt meet them returning." With that, he guided Margaret into a side path that led back toward the bottom of the garden.

They walked for a while in silence. Margaret was too frightened to speak, and Sir Justin was beginning to be bored. He had not believed that any young woman could be as bland and spiritless as Margaret Mayfield had appeared at the dinner table. But given the opportunity to exhibit some liveliness, she remained disgustingly insipid. He started to regret his impulse to tease her.

"You were in London for the season, I believe, Miss Mayfield?" he said finally to break the silence.

Margaret fleetingly raised huge blue eyes, then dropped them again, nodding.

"Did you enjoy yourself?"

These commonplace remarks, which might have set another girl more at ease, merely increased Margaret's agitation. Why was this man talking to her so? What did he plan? It must be something horrible. Her mother had assured her that he was capable of nothing else.

When she did not answer him, Keighley sighed. Miss Mayfield was, unbelievably, even more tedious than her parents. There was no sport in baiting such a creature. "Perhaps we should go back . . ." he started to say when, in his view, the girl abruptly went mad, clawing at his arm and gabbling hysterically.

For Margaret had suddenly, so she thought, divined his purpose in luring her away from the others. Ahead of them, just around the bend in the path, was the old summerhouse, a slightly tumbledown, disused building that Mr. Mayfield had recently locked up because of some misconduct on the part of a footman and a chambermaid. Margaret did not precisely understand what their sin had been, but she knew it was heinous, and she did not doubt that Keighley had brought her here for the same purpose. "Let me *go*," she gasped, tugging ineffectually at his arm.

Astonished, Sir Justin did so.

Margaret, by now beyond reason, pulled violently away from him, dislodging her cloak from her shoulders. She let it fall and started to run, thinking only of escape. But in her confusion she ran toward the summerhouse rather than away from it, and in a moment found herself backed against its door, desperate.

"Miss Mayfield?" called Keighley. "What is the matter?" His voice held only bewilderment, but Margaret was incapable of noticing. As he rounded the curve in the path and confronted her, she could think of only one thing to do. If she could somehow open the summerhouse door and get inside, she could relock it and scream for help. Surely they would come for her before he could get in. She turned and scrabbled at the door. The lock was new, but it appeared that someone had been tampering with it, for after a moment something slipped and the door opened. Margaret gasped with relief. "Miss Mayfield?" said a deep voice just behind her. She gave a little shriek and thrust herself through the doorway, tearing the shoulder of her gown on the frame. But before she could slam the door again and lock it, the man was upon her. He put one hand on the door and said, "What is it? What is wrong? Are you ill?"

"Leave me alone," cried Margaret, stumbling back into the building. She caught her heel on an uneven floorboard and started to fall, her arms flailing about violently. The shoulder of her dress parted, and as she jerked to pull it closed again her head struck the corner of a small table behind her, and she crumpled, insensible, to the floor.

Sir Justin bent over her, concerned and still bewildered. He felt her wrist for a pulse, then, hurriedly, her throat. There it was; she wasn't dead, at least. Her skirts had tumbled above her knees in the fall, and the man started to smooth them when he was interrupted by a babble of voices outside. Before he could move, he was transfixed by the beam of a lantern, and the rest of the dinner party peered in at him.

"My God," shrieked Mrs. Mayfield. Maria Twitchel looked shocked to the core, and her husband's prominent eyes nearly popped. Philip Manningham whitened and drew back a little while Squire Camden seemed to try to gather his wits.

"Sir," exclaimed Ralph Mayfield, who held the lantern. "What have you done to my daughter?"

Sitting back on his heels, Sir Justin Keighley cursed

vividly, drawing another shriek from his hostess and shocked glances from his fellow guests. Realizing that his hand still touched Margaret's skirts, he removed it and stood, towering over the group at the door. "Absolutely nothing," he replied, with a touch of hauteur.

"Do you really expect me to believe that?" Mr. Mayfield looked apoplectic.

Gazing from one to the other of his audience, Keighley almost sighed. "No," he said. "I don't suppose I do, really."

2

A half hour of complete chaos followed. Margaret was carried inside to her bedroom and revived, though she remained groggy and confused by her mother's noisy lamentations. The dinner guests, except Sir Justin, were sent home, the Twitchels nearly bursting with furtive excitement. Philip Manningham, still very pale, retreated to his own chamber soon after, leaving Ralph Mayfield alone in the library with Keighley.

Standing with his hands clasped behind him, his back to the empty fireplace, Mr. Mayfield looked distinctly nervous. But he summoned all his resolution and said, "Well, Sir Justin, what have you to say for yourself, eh?"

"Just this." And Keighley told him the whole story of his stroll with Margaret, omitting nothing.

"Hah," replied Mayfield when he had finished. He pondered a moment. "You expect me to believe that? That my daughter suddenly became hysterical for no reason and that the whole incident was her fault?"

Keighley shrugged. "I have told you what happened. I don't blame the girl. Perhaps I inadvertently said something to upset her. But I assure you I did not——"

"You do not blame *Margaret!*" Mr. Mayfield's uneasiness was forgotten in his anger. "Extraordinary! I find my daughter unconscious in the arms of a known rake, and he tells me he does not blame *her*. Well, sir, neither do I! I never dreamed of doing so. I hold you alone responsible, and I insist that you make amends for your scandalous attack on an innocent girl. I don't know what you may be accustomed to, but Margaret is not an unprotected female."

Keighley raised one black brow. "Amends?"

Mr. Mayfield glared at him.

"Can you possibly mean . . ."

"You know perfectly well what I mean. You must marry my daughter as soon as possible, to stop the talk that has no doubt already begun. Maria Twitchel will lose no time in spreading the story of what she saw tonight. But if we immediately announce an engagement and a wedding date, perhaps . . ."

Sir Justin's face was stony. "Have I not seen a betrothal announcement for your daughter? Last month?"

Mr. Mayfield made a despairing gesture. "That is at an end now, of course. Philip will not care to be married to a girl who has been publicly compromised."

"Will he not?" Keighley's lip curled.

"We could not expect it." sighed the other. "But as Margaret must marry you, it is of no—"

"Let me understand you. You consider me the sort of man who would violently assault a young gentlewoman, to the point of knocking her unconscious and tearing her clothes at an ordinary dinner party, and yet you insist that I marry your daughter?"

Mayfield's cheeks flushed slightly. "Much against my principles and inclination, I think it unavoidable, yes."

"You would sacrifice the girl without hesitation to some ridiculous notion of propriety?"

"I do not consider the rules of society ridiculous, sir," replied Ralph Mayfield stiffly. "Our moral code requires that—"

"*Your* moral code," echoed Sir Justin. "For my part, I flatly refuse."

His host gaped at him. "What?"

"I refuse to go along with this ludicrous scheme. I haven't the slightest desire to marry your daughter, nor she me if her behavior is any measure. I did *not* attack her, and I consider her honor unspotted as far as I am concerned. I won't do it." He rose, gazing down at the astounded Mayfield with a slight, ironic smile.

"You . . . you will leave my daughter to be disgraced?" gasped the older man. "You will abandon her, her reputation ruined, her name a byword among—"

"Oh, take a damper, Mayfield. If you and your wife had not made such a Cheltenham tragedy of this matter, we might have passed it off as the trifle it was. Did it occur to you to ask, 'Did she fall?' when you came upon us in your summerhouse? No, you immediately assumed the worst, as you supposedly 'moral' people always do, and cried 'Unhand my daughter.' Well, your narrow-mindedness is simply not my responsibility. You will do as you please, of course, but if I were you, I would tell the gossips the truth. Miss Mayfield tripped and fell, and I was trying to help her."

"Only an idiot would believe that," sputtered Mayfield.

"Indeed?" Sir Justin eyed him with icy contempt. "From what I have seen of your friends, that should cause no difficulty. Good evening." He turned on his heel and went out, leaving Ralph Mayfield speechless with shock and outrage.

In the meantime, upstairs, Mrs. Mayfield had been talking somewhat incoherently to her daughter. Margaret was not feeling well. Her head hurt abominably, it was very late, and she wanted to sleep. And she was still emotionally shaken by her supposed ordeal in the garden. These things, combined with Mrs. Mayfield's rambling monologue, prevented her from understanding what her

mother was talking about for quite a time. At last,
however, when she lamented, "To have to marry such a
man," for the fourth time, Margaret's eyes widened. "What
are you talking about, Mama?"

Mrs. Mayfield wrung her hands. "About Sir Justin,
dear. It pains me terribly to give you to such a man. I
thought your future, such a different future, so admirably
settled, and now *this*."

"I don't understand." Margaret tried to sit up straighter
on her pillows but sank back with a moan, putting a hand
to her injured head.

Her mother looked surprised. "But what else have we
been talking of this half hour? You must marry Sir Justin
now, of course, after what happened. It is dreadful,
but—"

"*M-marry*," Margaret gasped. She stared at her mother
in horror.

"I know you cannot like it, dear, but—"

"*Like* it? I cannot *do* it. I never want to see him again
as long as I live! He is horrible, despicable. I am afraid
of him."

"He is certainly not the sort of man we would have
chosen for you. But after what happened tonight, we have
no choice. You are compromised, Margaret. You must
marry him."

"Mama, I *cannot*. I . . . I hate him."

"I understand your feelings. He has acted in a way
even I would not have expected. When you are married,
however, he must treat you with that . . ."

Despite the pain, Margaret struggled upright. "Mama,
you cannot mean this. You are not serious. You *could* not
make me marry that man, after what he did to me."

Mrs. Mayfield shook her head mournfully. "I wish I
need not, Margaret. But you must understand that this
incident has destroyed your reputation. To be seen in
such a compromising position by a number of people,

practically strangers. The story will be common property in a week. The only way to scotch it is with a marriage. Your father's political position . . ."

"*His* position? What about mine? How could I live as *his* wife?"

"You might have thought of that before you slipped away alone with him," retorted her mother, who was becoming incensed with Margaret's unusual resistance. Her daughter had never before opposed her will.

"Slipped away?" Margaret gazed at her in outrage.

"Well, dear, you know that such behavior only encourages the kind of insult you received tonight. Sir Justin was in the wrong, of course, but he could not have, er, interfered with you if you had not given him the opportunity."

For an instant Margaret almost felt guilty for having dropped back from the group after dinner, then a quite unaccustomed rage rose in her docile breast. "That isn't true!" she cried. "I did not give him any opportunities. I did *nothing*. And I will never marry him. I *hate* him."

"Margaret, do not talk to me in that tone." Mrs. Mayfield was more startled than alarmed at her daughter's defiance.

"I won't marry him. I *won't*." Margaret buried her head in her pillows.

Her mother started to speak, then paused. "You are exhausted," she answered finally. "Try to sleep. We will talk in the morning."

There was no reply. Margaret was fighting tears and a growing terror. Disobeying her parents' wishes was nearly as frightening as what they wanted her to do. She was overcome by the strong emotions of this new dilemma.

Mrs. Mayfield gazed at her muffled form for a moment, a spark of something like sympathy in her rather hard eyes, then left the room and walked downstairs to the library. There she found her husband alone. "Has Sir

Justin gone already?" she asked. "I supposed I would find him still with you. Ralph, I'm afraid we have a problem. Margaret is insisting that she will not marry Keighley. We can bring her round, of course, but it may take a little—"

"It doesn't signify," replied Mr. Mayfield wearily. "He categorically refuses to have *her*."

His wife's mouth dropped open. "What?"

"He won't offer for her. Told me some rigmarole about Margaret's running from him and falling, for no reason. Patently false, of course, but he says he won't marry. He walked out on me."

"We must *make* him."

"How do you propose to do that? We have no influence with such a man. He doesn't even like us."

Mrs. Mayfield drew herself up alarmingly. "I shall go and talk to him, first thing tomorrow. He can't get away with this, not with *my* daughter."

Her husband shrugged. "You may try, certainly. But he won't listen to you."

"He must." The couple's eyes met for a long moment. "What will we do if he does not, Ralph?"

He shrugged again. "I suppose young Philip . . ."

"Will withdraw, of course. What would you do?"

Mr. Mayfield seemed uneasy about this question. "Perhaps we could find someone else to take her."

His wife laughed harshly. "A nobody? A tuft hunter satisfied with *our* consequence? No, it must be Keighley. It is his *duty*."

"He does not think so."

"I shall make him."

Mr. Mayfield looked skeptical, but he said only, "I hope you may, my dear."

Margaret did not fall asleep when her mother left her; she was far too upset. She tossed and turned in the bed like an animal caught in a trap and wondered what she could do. She knew she had not moved her mother. Tomorrow both her parents would exert their authority, and as she had never resisted it in her life before, she could not imagine doing so now. She would have to marry Sir Justin Keighley.

This thought drew a small moan. She could not! She really did hate and fear the man. Her feelings toward him were stronger than any she had ever experienced. Indeed, he seemed, in one short evening, to have turned her whole life upside down. What she was feeling now was immeasurably more intense than anything she had known. Her anger at her mother, her obstinant certainty about what she did *not* want, her fear for the future—all were dauntingly exaggerated. Her mind whirled with the violence of her own reactions. What was happening to her?

It was at this moment that she thought of Philip. For some reason he had been absent from her thoughts throughout this awful evening, but now he recurred, and Margaret at once felt a vast relief. Philip would save her. They were, after all, engaged. He had said he admired and respected her. Surely all would be well again if she married him, as she had meant to do, instead of . . . She shuddered; she could not even think his name.

Margaret breathed a great sigh. Why had her mother not thought of this solution? It was so easy and simple. But it didn't matter. *She* had thought of it, and first thing tomorrow morning she would speak to Philip. Then everything would be just as it had been, and she could go back to living her quiet, tranquil life and not worry about these new, frightening feelings. They were all Sir Justin Keighley's fault. Margaret could not understand what he had done to her, but she knew where the blame lay. If she could only thrust the man out of her life, everything would be peaceful again.

Margaret relaxed and wiggled into a comfortable position under the bedclothes. Now she could sleep, but she would be sure to wake early and catch Philip before the others came down. That way, it would all be settled before her parents could open the subject again.

All the members of the Mayfield household were up betimes the following day. Both Mr. and Mrs. Mayfield had slept badly and woke early and irascible. Their houseguest, Philip Manningham, rose to begin packing his things, for he foresaw that his visit would soon become awkward. Margaret was out of bed as soon as it was light, and though her head still gave her some pain, she was washed and dressed by the time her maid brought early tea. She drank it with dogged determination, as if it were medicine, then went out into the corridor and approached Philip's door. With the morning had come certain doubts about her plan, and great trepidation about this moment. Margaret would never before have imagined knocking at a man's bedchamber. Only desperation made her do so now, and immediately she began conjuring up awful possibilities. What if Philip were asleep or not yet fully dressed?

These fears dissolved when he opened the door, completely clothed and obviously wide awake. But the shock and amazement on his face when he saw her were almost as bad. Margaret's cheeks crimsoned. "Ph-Philip," she stammered, "I must talk to you. Could you come to the, er, library?"

His face showed nothing. "I'm rather busy. Can't it wait?"

His cold indifference nearly discouraged her, but the alternative was so terrible that Margaret managed to say, "It's important."

Philip looked annoyed. "Very well." He came into the hall, carefully shutting the door behind him, and started toward the stairs. Margaret, after a moment's hesitation, hurried after him. They did not speak until they reached the empty library. Then Philip said, "Well?"

Margaret's plan was crumbling around her. She could see that Philip's attitude toward her had changed. Though he had never been an ardent lover, he had treated her kindly and always had a ready smile. Now he did not seem to want to look at her. But once again the threat of the future forced her on. "You . . . you know what happened yesterday," she began.

"I could hardly help it."

"Yes. Well . . . well, Mama is saying that I must *marry* Sir Justin." She gazed at him with huge, appealing eyes.

Philip nodded. "Very right. It is the only possible solution, though distasteful, of course."

"B-but I am engaged to you," wailed Margaret, all her careful arguments falling away in the face of his agreement.

He stiffened. "You must realize, Margaret, that after what occurred here last night I cannot be expected to continue that connection. I am very sorry, naturally, but . . ."

"You are breaking it off?" Margaret sounded dazed.

"I should think your parents would have told you how it would be," he replied, almost angry. "It is not my fault. I did nothing."

"I thought you wished to marry me."

"So I did. It was a good match for us both. But you must see that it is impossible now. I am to have a seat in Parliament next election. I cannot have a wife who . . . Well, you understand."

"I thought you would help me. I cannot marry that man. If we married instead, would it not . . ."

Philip looked horrified. He backed away a few steps. "You are not seriously suggesting . . . It would ruin my career. No one could expect me to . . . This is all Keighley's fault. *He* is the one who must make amends. It is your duty to marry him, Margaret." The look in her blue eyes was too piteous to be ignored. "I know you don't like the idea now, but I daresay it won't be so bad. Keighley is considered very attractive to women, you know. They flock around him in London. And he has a tidy fortune. You'll be quite comfortable."

"*Comfortable*." She sounded revolted.

"You needn't look at me that way. I'm not to blame for this. No one can say that—"

"Of course they cannot," interrupted Margaret harshly. "Forgive me for expecting anything whatever. Good-bye, Philip." She fled in a rustle of skirts, leaving her former fiancé gazing uneasily after her. He waited a few minutes to be sure she was gone, then returned to his room and his packing. The sooner he got away, the better.

In her bedchamber Margaret sat numbly in the window-seat and wondered what she was to do. Her mother would come up very soon and reopen the question of her marriage to Justin Keighley. She would not be able to resist her for long. Then they would bring *him* here again, and she would be expected to accept his offer. Margaret leaped to her feet. She *couldn't*. She really couldn't. Running to her wardrobe, she pulled out a bandbox and began to stuff a few necessities into it. Her only hope was to run away.

When she had packed what she thought she could carry, Margaret went to the door and softly opened it. There was no one in the corridor. Taking the bandbox and a cloak, she crept out and hurried to the head of the stairs, where she stood listening for a long moment before running down them. The front hall was also empty. She was at the front door when she thought of something that made her cheeks pale. She hesitated, then ran to the library just down the hall; she slipped in, took a certain object, and the next minute was outside and away. She would get one of the stableboys to saddle her horse. She could think of a story that would satisfy him. And before anyone noticed she had gone, she would be well away.

She was halfway to the stables when she realized that she had no idea where to go. Who would shelter her in this dreadful situation? Margaret quickly reviewed her various relations; there was not one who would not return her immediately to her parents. She thought of her London acquaintances. No help there, either. She put a hand to her breast as she realized that for the first time in her short life she was alone. She trembled, and almost turned back. She could not manage by herself. Then she stiffened a bit and tried to think. Was there nowhere she could go?

London was out of the question. Too many people would recognize her there; besides, she was frightened of the crowds. No, she would not go east. This decision led naturally to its opposite, and she suddenly recalled Penzance. She and her mother had visited that town several times when an old aunt was ill there. The woman had since died, but Margaret was familiar with the place and loved it. She would go west to Penzance, and once there . . . Well, she would worry over that when the time came. With a slight nod, she continued on her way to the stables.

3

Margaret's plan was not really a very clever one. She had had little experience with any sort of subterfuge, and it was immediately apparent to Mrs. Mayfield, when she entered her daughter's room less than a quarter hour after the girl had left it, that something was wrong. A hasty examination of the wardrobe told her all, and she hurried to lay her discovery before her husband in the breakfast room.

"Run away?" exclaimed Ralph Mayfield. *"Margaret?"*

His wife was working her fingers into a pair of ivory kid gloves. She had been dressed to go out for some time. "I know it seems unbelievable, but Margaret was under a great strain. We must send to the stables, of course, to make sure, but I am satisfied that she has gone."

"What shall we do? I must go after her, I suppose. But where?"

"I don't think so," answered Mrs. Mayfield.

"What do you mean?"

"I think we should wait for the outcome of my talk with Sir Justin."

"You still intend to go?"

"Yes, indeed."

"And Margaret?

"An hour or two will make no difference. She may even have second thoughts and return in that time. In any case she hasn't the sense or the courage to run far. We can fetch her when we like."

Mr. Mayfield looked doubtful. "Something might happen to her. I don't like to think of her out on the roads alone."

"Something already *has* happened to her," replied his wife brusquely. "And now I must go and see what I can do about it. I shouldn't be long." She swept out into the hall and to her waiting barouche, leaving her husband frowning into his coffee cup.

Sir Justin Keighley, though a late riser in town, was always out of bed early in the country, and he had already breakfasted and was about to go out riding when Mrs. Mayfield arrived. He greeted her with annoyed resignation, but no surprise, and ushered her into his study. He had known that he had not heard the last of the Mayfield affair and anticipated facing Mrs. Mayfield before it was over, a confrontation he felt fully able to dominate.

"You know, of course, why I have come," the lady began.

Keighley bowed his head in acknowledgment.

"My husband has told me your story and your position. I must say I am disappointed in you, Sir Justin."

One corner of his mouth turned up. "Surely not. From what I have gathered of your opinion of me, it must have been just what you expected."

Mrs. Mayfield met his hazel eyes stonily. "I never thought you without honor."

He inclined his head ironically again. "We won't dispute the point, since it does not enter here."

"You do not think your treatment of my daughter . . ."

"Mrs. Mayfield, if your husband indeed told you my 'story,' you know that I did nothing whatever to your daughter. I am sorry that she has been upset, but I haven't the faintest notion why."

"Considering the two personalities involved, that is rather difficult to believe, don't you think?"

"I don't know. I am barely acquainted with Miss Mayfield."

His guest drew herself up. "Do you dare to suggest . . ."

"I suggest nothing, except that you and your husband are making a great deal too much out of a trivial matter. I will not be forced to marriage over this, madam. You can be sure of that."

Meeting his gaze, Mrs. Mayfield realized she would not move him with accusations or threats. "Margaret has run away," she said.

"What?"

"Run away. I discovered it this morning."

"But why?"

Mrs. Mayfield debated with herself for a moment. Should she tell him the true reason? He would find that very amusing, no doubt. "Because we told her you refused to marry her," she answered. "She could not face the disgrace."

Sir Justin Keighley's hazel eyes flashed. "You stupid woman. How could you treat your own daughter so?"

Though she clenched her fists, Mrs. Mayfield held her temper in check. "I thought it best that she know the truth."

"Indeed? Well, I hope you see your mistake now. When Mayfield brings her back, you must—"

"Oh, we shan't go after her."

"I beg your pardon?"

"We will let her go. It seems best. She is irretrievably ruined." Though she did not look directly at Keighley when she said this, she watched his reaction from the corner of her eye.

"You cannot be serious."

Mrs. Mayfield shrugged. "What is she to do if she returns home? Margaret is not strong enough to face down gossip."

"You will abandon a girl of, what, eighteen or nineteen? Do you have any idea what is likely to happen to her?"

The woman shook her head and looked down. "I suppose it is God's will."

"God's . . ." He paused and surveyed her. "I don't believe it."

"What?"

"You have wrapped that girl in cotton wool since she was born. You won't let her go now."

Mrs. Mayfield met his eyes squarely. "There is nothing I can do for her. It would be more cruel to bring her back to face the world's scorn." She rose. "*I* am not to blame for my poor daughter's plight. You are. And you are the only one who can make amends."

"Nonsense," replied Keighley automatically. His mind appeared to be elsewhere. Mrs. Mayfield watched him carefully. "Where could she go?" he added. "To London?"

His guest's eyes glinted, though she kept her face impassive. "Oh, no. She has no friends there. I suppose she would go west."

"To Cornwall?"

"Yes. We have visited several times in Penzance."

"Ah. She has friends there, then." He seemed to relax a little.

"Not any longer." Keighley glanced sharply up at her, but Mrs. Mayfield was absorbed in pulling on her gloves. "I must go. Ralph is prostrate over this affair. He mustn't be left alone."

"Too ill to travel, I suppose?" said Sir Justin sarcastically.

"Much," agreed the other. "Good day." As she turned

away Mrs. Mayfield again examined him from the corner of her eye. What she saw seemed to satisfy her, and her expression as she left the house was much less unpleasant than when she arrived.

Keighley paced his study uneasily for several minutes after she had gone. Finally he leaned on the mantelpiece and tapped it with impatient fingers. "She can't have been telling me the truth," he said aloud. "They must go after the chit." He tapped his fingers and frowned, recalling all he knew about the Mayfields. They were the most pompous, stiff-necked, narrow-minded people he had ever encountered. Was it possible that they would abandon a daughter they believed disgraced, seeing that as the easiest way out? He could not quite reject the possibility.

That girl is no more fit to fend for herself than a lame sheep, he thought. He pictured various horrible fates that might befall her. I shouldn't have teased her. I could see that she wasn't up to it. He thought again of the previous evening, remembering Margaret's inexplicable behavior. She's practically half-witted, he concluded. Then, with a sigh half exasperated, half resigned, he rang for a servant. "Is my horse ready?" he asked when the bell was answered.

"Yes, sir, the groom has been waiting."

"Good. I have just remembered some business I must take care of. I may not return until late."

"Yes, sir."

Sir Justin strode out, and as he mounted his horse he thought that it would scarcely take more than a day for him to catch the girl and return her to her home, with a few choice words for her parents as he did so.

For the first hour Margaret had ridden in an agony of apprehension. The grooms had looked at her strangely when she settled her bandbox before her on the saddle, and she was terrified that they would fetch her mother to stop her or send someone in pursuit. But as the time passed and no one came she relaxed enough to allow other worries to intrude. When she had traveled down to Cornwall before, it had been by coach, so she had a hazy recollection of the roads, but she was afraid to ask the way of strangers. Indeed, the people she met, some of whom looked surprised to see a young lady riding unaccompanied with a parcel before her, were her chief concern. Novel reading and her mother's strictures had given her vivid pictures of what happened to lone women who had anything to do with unknown persons.

Yet no one accosted her, and gradually the beating of her heart slowed a bit. Perhaps she could manage this journey. She need only keep going west and south, and surely there would be signposts. When she reached Penzance . . . Here, Margaret faltered, but her memories of that town were so filled with sunshine and flowers that she could not believe she would have trouble there.

The July morning grew warm, and Margaret's blue cloth riding habit became oppressive. It also occurred to her that she had done nothing about food. Though she was only a little hungry now, she would have to get something to eat before the day was out, and that meant an inn, a prospect that made her quake. She had known that she could not make this journey in one day, but she had been putting off thinking of inns and other complications, concentrating on getting away from the neighborhood of home. Now she faced the fact that she would have to apply to strangers for shelter, and the idea made her heart start to pound again.

Always her parents, her governess, or some servant had been with her when she traveled, making all the arrangements and dealing with people. The only time she had spoken to strangers was during the season, and then she had said little to a few carefully screened by her mother. How could she engage a room for the night? What would she say? She trembled even imagining it.

This moment was probably the lowest of Margaret's whole life. Plodding along on her docile mare, wearily balancing the bandbox before her, she considered turning around and going home again. Perhaps it would be easier just to do what they asked. Perhaps marriage to Sir Justin would not be *too* dreadful. Yet the thought of it made her shiver, even in the July heat. And suddenly something happened to her. In the past twenty-four hours her life had been revolutionized. She had experienced feelings wholly alien to her, and she had taken action with a determination that astonished her, now that she thought about it. Here she was, riding along alone, and nothing dreadful had occurred. The sky had not fallen; passersby did not stare at her in horror. Perhaps, she thought, I can do more than I know. Perhaps I do not need Mama or the others to tell me how to go on.

For a while she turned this original idea over in her mind wonderingly. It was both exciting and frightening. Then it was dissipated by the abrupt realization that she was lost. The road ahead curved north. She had been riding steadily southwest for more than two hours and was confident that she had passed into Cornwall by this time, for their house was near the Devon border. Though Penzance was still miles away, she had felt she was making progress. To turn north would be disastrous. Yet her only other choice was a narrow, grassy lane that did not look at all well traveled. It probably led to a farm or village or was a dead end.

When she considered turning around and retracing her path, however, Margaret decided on the lane. At least it went in the right direction; she could not face losing ground. As it turned out, this was a wise decision, for the track soon connected with a larger road that looked vaguely familiar, and a signpost at the crossing told her that she had passed beyond Plymouth and was well into Cornwall. She was so elated by this discovery that she found the courage to halt at an inn and buy a supply of bread and cheese. Though she could not bring herself to remain there to eat it, this minor victory raised her spirits further, and she continued her journey happily into the afternoon.

Some miles behind her, Justin Keighley was in a far different humor. He had thought that finding a solitary young lady on the road would be relatively simple, and that it would be accomplished during the morning. But his inquiries had so far produced little helpful information. Two of the many people he had asked had seen a girl who must be Margaret, and these two were widely enough separated to convince him that he was indeed on the track. But her route appeared exasperatingly eccentric, for several idlers who should have seen her if she had taken the most direct way denied all knowledge of such a traveler. He had begun to regret his impulsive departure almost immediately, and by noontime, when he stopped at a roadside inn to eat, he had nearly decided to give up what he was beginning to characterize as a ridiculous quest.

Two things altered his mind. He got further news of Margaret from the innkeeper, who had sold her food not more than an hour since. And the gross talk and manners of a fellow diner reminded him of what could be in store for the girl if she was not brought back. He returned to the saddle physically refreshed and mentally hardened. He *would* find the chit, and he would take her home, with a scold that she should never forget.

The sun moved down the western sky, and the day grew hotter. The two travelers rode on at about the same pace, for Keighley was hampered by the necessity of making inquiries along the way. But at last, when he had been assured by four observers in a row that they had seen Margaret, he concluded that she was keeping to the coast road, which had bent down toward the eastern shore some time since, and he urged his horse forward. If his luck held, he would catch up with her before twilight. It was deuced awkward to be so far from home, but he would manage some acceptable arrangement for the night and get her back tomorrow. As he thought this, he cursed the girl again for her stupidity. He had never known such a bacon-brained female, and it would be very satisfying to tell her so to her face.

Margaret had given up the thought of pursuit and was actually enjoying the sight of the sea in the distance and the scent of flowers in the air, though the need to find a room for the night loomed before her. She was also very tired, never having ridden for so long before, and she had let her mare slow to a plodding walk. When she heard hoofbeats behind her, she did not even turn until they were quite close. But then a tremor of doubt shot through her and she looked, only to find her darkest fears realized. Sir Justin himself had come after her—and alone. At once her heart started to pound. She kicked her mount convulsively, startling that gentle animal into an awkward canter.

"Miss Mayfield," called Sir Justin sharply. "I have come to take you home. It is no use running farther."

His voice unsettled her so much that her grip on the bandbox loosened, and it fell into the road, bursting open and scattering her things in the dust. But she did not pause for an instant, merely kicking her mare again and holding the reins tightly as the combination of this unusual command and the fluttering in the road catapulted the horse into a wild gallop.

Keighley also urged his horse forward, and as it was much the more powerful mount, he was soon closing the distance between them. In a few moments they were abreast and he was leaning out to grasp her horse's head and pull both to a stop.

"*No*," cried Margaret, trying to fling herself down even before they stopped moving. "I won't go with you. Leave me alone."

Holding his own horse with his powerful knees, Keighley kept one hand on Margaret's reins and, with the other, imprisoned her left arm in an iron grip. "Don't be a fool," he snapped, "or try to be less of one, at any rate."

Margaret lost her head. Fumbling in the pocket of her gown, she drew out the pistol that she had taken from her father's drawer just before she left the house. She knew it was loaded; her mother was always complaining about it. "Let me go," she insisted, waving the gun in the air so that Keighley could see it.

"Where did you get that? Put it away at once and stop being ridiculous."

This seemed the last straw. After all she had been through, to be called a fool and ridiculous. She cocked the pistol as she had seen her father do and pointed it at him. "Let go of me and *go away*."

He jerked her other arm impatiently and started to speak, but the abrupt movement jostled the gun, and with a deafening roar it went off, leaving Margaret dazed and trembling. As she watched, frozen with horror, a red stain appeared on Keighley's left shoulder and spread. His initial look of astonishment altered to a grimace, his grip loosened, and slowly he bent and slipped from his horse into a heap on the road.

Margaret's mouth dropped open, and her blue eyes bulged. She hadn't meant to shoot him. She had just wanted to frighten him away, so that he would leave her alone. Drops of blood began to show in the dust beside Keighley's shoulder. His horse sidled uneasily and whickered. Somewhere in the field beside the road, a lark trilled. Margaret burst into frantic, desperate sobs.

4

Unable to stop crying, but knowing that she must do something if Sir Justin was not to bleed to death, Margaret struggled out of the saddle and dropped heavily to the ground. She went to Keighley and gingerly straightened his limbs until he was lying on his back in the road. The shoulder of his blue coat was now soaked with blood. Sniffling and wringing her hands, Margaret bent over him. She must stop the bleeding—she knew that much—and she must get help. But how? She had no knowledge of physic, and she couldn't leave him to find someone who did.

Gathering all her resolution, Margaret knelt in the dust and pulled open Keighley's coat, then his shirt. There was a small wound in the hollow of his left shoulder. She swallowed convulsively. *She* had done this. Thinking furiously, she seemed to remember that one stopped bleeding by pressing a cloth over the spot. Sir Justin's handkerchief was before her, and she hastily folded it into a pad and laid it over the wound. It was immediately wet through with blood.

With a sound between a gasp and a sob, Margaret took it away again, looked around like a hunted rabbit, then turned back the skirt of her riding habit and began to rip her petticoat into strips. Luckily it was made in tiers and easy to pull apart. When she had a wad of cambric, she again folded a pad and pressed it to Keighley's shoulder. To her immeasurable relief, it seemed to slow the bleeding.

"What be this?" asked a deep voice behind her, making Margaret start so that the bandage jerked free. Pressing it down again, she craned her neck and saw a countryman standing near the edge of the road. He had obviously approached across the field beyond. "Heerd a shot," he added, gazing apprehensively at the scene before him.

Margaret thought more rapidly than ever before in her life. Where was the pistol? She had dropped it, but she couldn't see it now. No, there it was, just hidden by the edge of her skirt. The man wouldn't notice it. "Highwaymen," she gasped. "They attacked us and took our luggage. My . . . my brother and I were riding to Penzance."

"Highwaymen?" The man seemed astounded. "We bain't had any sich thing hereabouts."

"Well, you do now," snapped Margaret, her fear making her brave. "Is there a house or a village nearby? My brother needs help. Could you go for someone, please?"

He scratched his head. "Closest village be yonder." He pointed toward the sea. "Down on the shore." He looked at Keighley doubtfully. "Path's steep, though."

"Could you fetch some men from there? He will have to be carried. Please hurry. I don't know anything about wounds, and I am . . ." She caught her breath with difficulty. "I am afraid this one may be serious."

"Village men be all out fishing," objected her companion.

"Then get someone else," she almost shrieked.

The man backed away a step, then bobbed his head and turned to hurry off on the other side of the road. In a few minutes he had disappeared over the cliff edge.

Quickly Margaret reached for the pistol and slipped it in the pocket of her gown.

"Please, God, let him get back in time," she murmured, pressing down on the bandage with all the strength of her tiring fingers.

It seemed years before anyone came, though it was not more than twenty minutes before a group of people emerged from the cliff path and hurried toward her—four women led by the countryman and another burly male.

"Tch, tch," said the latter when they came close. "What's all this, then?" And without waiting to find out, he knelt beside Margaret and replaced her fingers with his on the bandage. With a tremulous sigh, she sat back. "Highwaymen, is it?" continued the stranger. "We've hardly heard of such a thing in these parts. Terrible."

Margaret gazed up mutely at the group surrounding her. A sturdy middle-aged woman stepped forward and nodded. "I'm Mrs. Appleby," she said. "That's my husband." She indicated the kneeling man. "We keep a tavern in the village. Dan's the only man about today. Fishing boats are out."

"Do you have a room?" asked Margaret. "Can we take my . . . brother there? We must find him a doctor at once."

Mrs. Appleby looked doubtful. "I can give you rooms. We have one or two we let now and then. But as for a doctor—"

"Let's get him home, Flos, and worry over that later," interrupted her husband. "Here, you, Luke, help me carry him. We can do it between us. The young lady can hold the bandage as we go, and you girls lead the horses." Margaret noticed that the other three women were quite young and, from their looks, daughters of the Applebys.

The climb down to the village was harrowing. There was a road a mile or so ahead, they told Margaret, but the cliff path was much quicker. Unfortunately it was also rough and steep, and it was no easy task carrying an unconscious man down it while keeping a bandage in place. At last, however, they managed it, walked a few hundred yards along a level beach, and came to the village, a cluster of whitewashed cottages perched above a seawall. The tavern, the Red Lion, was the topmost building, its foundations even with the roof of the next level. They hurried Keighley inside and up a narrow staircase to a small, clean bedchamber with windows looking out to sea, and laid him on the bed, Mrs. Appleby hastily stripping off the white counterpane just in time.

Margaret breathed a great sigh as Mr. Appleby again took her place with the bandage. "Where does the doctor live?" she asked. "I will go myself; I am too worried to wait."

The Applebys shifted uneasily. "We don't have a doctor, properly speaking," replied the wife. "Not in the village. There's one in Falmouth, but that's more than an hour off, even at a gallop."

"But he *must* have a doctor."

"There's old Mrs. Dowling," offered one of the daughters. Mr. Appleby frowned.

"I reckon she'll have to do," said Mrs. Appleby slowly.

"Who is she?" asked Margaret.

"She's our midwife, like. She nurses in the village. She knows her business, miss. And there's no one else in reach."

Margaret wrung her hands. "I'd rather have a doctor."

Mrs. Appleby shrugged, though she looked sympathetic.

"Very well, ask Mrs. Dowling to come. But could someone ride to the doctor as well, please? Perhaps he could come tomorrow."

The Applebys looked skeptical but agreed, and one of the daughters was sent for the midwife. Margaret sat down in the room's solitary chair and gazed at Sir Justin.

He was terribly pale. Even his lips were bloodless, and his black brows stood out startlingly against his pallid skin. The bandage was showing spots of blood now, so the bleeding had not entirely stopped, and Margaret thought he looked dreadful. She gazed appealingly up at Mr. Appleby, who continued to hold the cloth in place on Keighley's shoulder. "Will he be all right, do you think?"

"Lord, miss, I've seen wounds worse than this heal in a matter of weeks," replied the man stoutly. "In the peninsula we had men torn up something fearful stout as ever in a month." His wife frowned a little, and he grimaced at her.

Margaret continued to stare at Keighley. "I hope he will be."

"Course he will, miss."

They sat in silence for a while. The two remaining daughters slipped out of the room, and a few minutes later, heavy footsteps sounded on the stairs and the third daughter ushered an elderly woman in. Margaret drew back a little at her appearance. Mrs. Dowling, for so this must be, looked exactly like Margaret's idea of a witch. She was old and a little bent, dressed in a shapeless gray gown, and her gray hair was twisted in a frizzled bun on her thin neck. She had a prominent nose and sunken blue eyes, which seemed to take in everything about her at a glance. Margaret hunched a bit.

But Mrs. Dowling's attention was directed at Keighley. "Is he really shot?" she asked Appleby. He nodded, and she pursed her lips, setting a bundle on the small bedside table. "Let's have a look, then." Appleby slowly removed his hands and stepped back as Mrs. Dowling took his place. She peeled back the pad and gazed at the hole in Keighley's shoulder. "Tch, tch, bullet still in, I suppose."

"Seems so," agreed Appleby.

Mrs. Dowling sighed and opened her bundle, taking

out some implements, which filled Margaret with dread. "Who's the young lady?" inquired the midwife.

"Sister."

"Ah. You'd best go downstairs, dearie."

Margaret knew she should protest, should insist upon staying and helping with the operation. But she couldn't bear the thought of watching Mrs. Dowling use those pinchers on Sir Justin. Mutely she nodded and turned to go. "I'll speak to you after," added the old woman. "We'll need some boiling water, Flos."

"It'll be on by now. I'll fetch it up."

The two walked downstairs together. "You can sit in the front parlor, miss. There's no one about this time of day."

"Thank you." Margaret entered the indicated room and sat down on an old brown sofa. She clasped her hands in her lap and endeavored to wait calmly. But the awful scene in the road kept running through her mind, and she was oppressed with a dreadful sense of guilt. What if Sir Justin died? It would be she who had killed him. She had never meant to hurt him. And if he recovered, as she profoundly hoped he would, how angry he was going to be.

These dismal thoughts led to others. If—*when*—he felt better, how were they to go on? It was obvious that he would not be traveling for a long while, and she could not, of course, abandon him here. But what were they to do for clothes or money? All her things were scattered on the road, and the small amount of money she had been able to scrape together, though safe in a packet in her reticule, would not last them long.

Margaret put her forehead in her hand and fought tears once again. She had never felt so miserable. Her former placid existence seemed a vast distance away as well as incalculably desirable now that it was gone forever. For some time she lost herself in a self-pitying haze.

A sound from the doorway brought her upright with a jerk. Mrs. Dowling stood there, gazing at her and looking even more disturbingly like a fairy-tale witch. "Is he all right?" asked Margaret.

The old woman came farther into the parlor and shut the door. "I got the bullet," she answered. "But he's weak. Hasn't come round yet. He'll need nursing." She surveyed Margaret skeptically.

"I . . . I'll nurse him, if you will tell me exactly what I must do."

Mrs. Dowling laughed shortly. "I can do that all right. But I doubt you'll relish the job."

"I can do what I must," answered Margaret, wondering as she said the words whether they were true.

"Can ye, now?" The other seemed to weigh this statement. "What's your name, girl?"

"Oh, I'm sorry. It's Margaret . . . Margaret, er, Camden." She used the first name that came into her head as she suddenly realized that she did not wish to reveal her own.

"And the gentleman?"

"He's my brother . . . Harry Camden."

"To be sure, they told me he was your brother." Her sharp blue eyes bored into Margaret's. "You're not much alike."

"N-no. I resemble my mother and he our father." She was amazed at her own inventiveness. Falsehoods seemed to flow from her tongue automatically.

"Indeed? Well, it's lucky for him he has a sister here, for he's in a bad way, and no mistake. You'll be sending to your parents, likely?"

"Er, no. They're . . . traveling abroad."

Mrs. Dowling folded her thin arms over her chest and gazed at Margaret. The girl moved uneasily. "Huh," said the midwife finally. "Well, if you really mean to take on the nursing . . ."

"I do."

"Come along, then, and I'll show you what must be done."

Relieved to be finished with questions, Margaret followed her up the stairs and back to Keighley's bedchamber. He was lying on his back again, his shirt gone and his shoulder swathed in strips of linen. His breathing sounded ominously heavy to Margaret. But Mrs. Dowling ignored it, merely giving rapid instructions before packing up her bundle once again. "I'll be by tomorrow," she finished. "And I live just down the way. Send if he seems bad."

"Yes, thank you. Thank you very much, Mrs. Dowling. I don't know what we should have done without you. Do we, er, owe you . . ."

"Wait until he begins to mend, then we'll talk of payment."

"Thank you." Margaret was relieved at this.

The old woman nodded and turned to go, hitching her bundle onto her hip. "You'd best send for someone," she said over her shoulder. "Nursing's no light task, and I have other calls."

"I'll manage."

Mrs. Dowling shrugged unbelievingly and went out.

Left alone with the unconscious Keighley, Margaret began to wonder what made her think she could manage. She had never managed anything without her mother in nineteen years. Perhaps she should send for help. But who? Not her parents. Margaret shuddered at the thought of telling them what had befallen her. If they had wished her to marry Sir Justin *before*, what must they say now? And they would never forgive her for shooting him, even by mistake.

What of Sir Justin's connections, though? Not his family—the mere thought of contacting any of them made Margaret cringe. She could not possibly explain what had occurred. But what of his servants? She could write to his house and ask someone to come. But then the neighborhood would know where he was, and the servant would recognize her and tell her parents. No, that would not do, either. It appeared things were up to her.

Margaret drooped guiltily. The situation was very bad, and no doubt all her fault. She had certainly made a mull of it when she took her life into her own hands. How could she assume the responsibility for another's? She looked again at Keighley. He still breathed stertorously; his skin was deathly pale. She hadn't killed him yet, but she might with her unskilled nursing. A wave of hopelessness washed over Margaret; she felt like giving up.

But at that low moment, when all her resources seemed gone, some spark of obstinacy sprang to life, and Margaret raised her head. She had made a great many mistakes but, after all, she had no experience in managing. No one got a thing right all at once. If she persevered, would she not improve? And everything was *not* her fault. Sir Justin, at least, shared the guilt. She would show him— she would show them all—that she was not the little fool they thought her. She would nurse Justin Keighley back to health, and then she would go . . . Her plan did not extend further at the moment. She would think of something.

With a new determination visible in the set of her shoulders and the expression on her face, Margaret rose and poured out a glass of barley water from the jug standing on the night table. She was supposed to get Keighley to drink as much of it as he would. She might as well start.

5

The terrible night that followed broke down Margaret's resolution. Though she was shown another neat bedchamber by Mrs. Appleby and lent a crisp nightdress by one of her daughters, she made no use of either. For Keighley showed signs of increasing illness through the evening, and she was afraid to leave him after dinner. He did not regain consciousness, but he thrashed about in the bed muttering incoherent phrases, obviously in great pain. And his forehead, when she touched it, seemed on fire. Alone in the empty hours of early morning, while everyone in the village slept, Margaret concluded that she could not face another such time. She would have to find help. She knew nothing of nursing, and it seemed to her that Keighley must die of his wound if he were left to her care. Indeed, she was terrified once or twice in the night that he *was* dying.

Soon after dawn, Mrs. Appleby tapped on the door with a pot of steaming tea. "How is he?" she whispered, shaking her head at Keighley's appearance and at Margaret's.

"Not good," replied the girl. "I really think we must send someone for the doctor as soon as possible. I don't know what to do for him."

Mrs. Appleby nodded. "My youngest son will be home today. He's been visiting his grandmother. He can ride to Falmouth."

"Thank you."

The older woman eyed her. "You haven't slept, miss. I told you to call me if you needed someone to watch him."

"I didn't like to trouble you. And in any case . . ."

"Well, me or one of my girls will sit with him now. You must eat something and then sleep a bit. It won't help matters if you make yourself ill."

Wearily Margaret agreed. Keighley had quieted with the coming of dawn. "But I am too restless to sleep," she replied. "I think I will go out and walk a little. I shan't be long."

"You must take some breakfast first."

"Perhaps when I come back. But if one of you could sit with . . . my brother, I would be very grateful."

Mrs. Appleby nodded, looking concerned, and in a few moments Margaret found herself outside the tavern door, in a borrowed shawl, and looking down over the roofs of the village. Gilded with sunrise, they looked almost beautiful, and she stood still a moment to watch the morning brighten above the sea. It was a clear summer day, with the promise of heat.

Finding a pathway—half alley, half stair—leading down, she walked the short distance to the seawall, which was a sturdy gray stone construction rising fifteen feet above the beach. A cobbled road behind the top curved around the village and back inshore on either side; at the bottom a narrow stretch of sand was washed by small waves.

Margaret took deep breaths of the sea air and soon found herself enough refreshed to appreciate the beauty of her surroundings. Her parents' land in Devon was in the midst of rich green farm country, and it was lovely. But this was a different landscape, one that attracted her more. She walked the whole half circle of the seawall.

Nearly every house had a small garden planted with flowering shrubs and vines that clambered over the walls and roofs. The warming sun caused their scents to fill the air. As she stood at the shore and looked up, the whole village seemed like some fairy-tale castle of white tiers and blossoms.

Margaret strolled about for more than an hour before she guiltily remembered her responsibilities and returned to the Red Lion, where she found a plentiful breakfast waiting, and Mrs. Appleby insisted she eat before going up to Keighley again. "Jemmy got back just now," she told the girl. "I sent him along for the doctor. Can't expect them before afternoon, but I've hopes they'll come then." She grimaced. "I've sent word there's a *gentleman* ill—that should bring him."

Margaret looked anxious.

"Don't you be worriting. Annie's with him now. She nursed her sisters and brothers through the ague two winters ago. She's a fine nurse. Never lost a one, we didn't."

This sounded hopeful. "Do you think," ventured Margaret, "that she would be willing to share the nursing with me? I would pay her something, of course, for her trouble."

"You must ask her that. But I'm sure she'd be willing. And a bit of extra money wouldn't come amiss. Annie's to marry Jack Thompson in the autumn and set up her own house."

"I'll ask her at once," said Margaret, rising from the table. "Thank you for all your help, Mrs. Appleby."

"It's little we've done. You should have fetched me in the night. I meant to wake on my own, but I was that tired."

"It was all right," Margaret lied.

"Shall we have Mrs. Dowling again before the doctor?"

"She said she would come today."

"Ah." Mrs. Appleby started to clear off the table. "I've put some broth on the hob. Perhaps the gentleman can take some later on."

"Yes, thank you." Margaret returned to Keighley's room to find him much the same as when she left. A brief conference with Annie established her willingness to help with the nursing, and they made arrangements to divide the time. Margaret was impressed with the girl's calm competence. Though they were probably about the same age, Annie seemed much better equipped to deal with the situation.

By the time they finished, Mrs. Dowling had arrived to check her patient. Her assessment was more optimistic than Margaret expected, though she was not offended to hear that the doctor had been sent for. "A bit of fever's bound to come with that sort of wound," she assured Margaret. "Might last awhile, too. Never can tell. He looks a strong man, though. He'll do. Don't let the doctor bleed him, mind."

"*Bleed* him—he has lost too much blood already."

Mrs. Dowling chuckled, her shrewd blue eyes twinkling. "These doctors have their ways, miss. Perhaps I'll come by while he's here." She looked at Margaret sidelong.

"Yes, indeed, you should. You can tell him more than I about the wound."

The midwife seemed surprised but pleased. However, she replied only, "Keep the wet cloths on his head and let him drink whenever he will. And don't worry, child, he's not like to die."

Margaret reminded herself of this last several times during the course of the morning. Sir Justin did not thrash as much as he had in the night; on the contrary, he lay almost too still and breathed heavily and loudly. Every so often his black brows would draw together and he would murmur a few words, but she could never understand them. His forehead, when she changed the cloth, was always hot.

Mrs. Appleby brought up a tray around one, and with it some news. "One of the lads found some ladies' clothes and things scattered on the cliff road a mile or so off. I thought they might be yours, Miss Camden, so I told him to bring them here."

"Oh, yes." Recollecting herself, Margaret added, "Was there a bandbox? And a . . . a blue dress?"

"I don't know, miss. I'll call you when the things arrive."

"Oh, yes, thank you. Perhaps the . . . the highwaymen dropped some of our luggage."

Nodding skeptically, Mrs. Appleby went out. Margaret turned to her luncheon tray and poured out a cup of tea from the pot. The food she left; she was not hungry after her substantial breakfast.

She was just getting a second cup, and gazing out the window at the sea, when a weak voice murmured, *"You."* Turning, she found Keighley's hazel eyes open and regarding her.

"You're awake. How do you feel?"

The man ignored this and continued to stare at her. Slowly Margaret's face crimsoned. "Where are we?" croaked Sir Justin.

"A . . . a village. A tavern. Th-the owners are very nice."

"Cornwall?"

"Y-yes." She wondered if he were still off his head. Where else could they be?

"And is my memory possibly correct? Did you, in fact, shoot me?" His tone was coldly scornful.

"It was an *accident*."

He closed his eyes for a moment, then opened them again. "You pointed a pistol at me and fired. Hardly a description of an accident."

"I was only trying to frighten you away. I didn't mean to hurt you."

Sir Justin's chest rose and fell under the coverlet. He seemed to gather his energy before replying, "You are the most witless, whimpering ninnyhammer it has ever been my misfortune to encounter, even in a long series of London seasons, which abound in the species. Through your inexplicable, idiotic antics, I have been bored, annoyed, and now confined to a lumpy bed, in what appears to be a common alehouse, with a pistol ball in my shoulder. I am enduring considerable pain, and I suppose I will not be able to leave for some time. I can only hope that you are satisfied with this and do not contemplate any further mayhem. What are you doing here, by the by? I would have expected you to seize the opportunity to flee."

Stung, her cheeks hot, Margaret retorted, "I wish I *had* left you on the road. But since my shooting you *was* an accident, I of course summoned help and brought you to the nearest shelter. And if you think so little of me, I wonder that you came after me at all. Why did you not simply let me be?"

"Would that I had." Keighley shifted his weight and winced. "I must have taken leave of my senses to let a woman like your mother maneuver me into pursuit."

"M-mama?"

"Yes. I can see now that it was just what she hoped for. Of course she would have sent someone else if I had not taken the bait."

"She is not coming after you?"

He laughed shortly. "Oh, no. Your parents have abandoned you to your fate, according to her."

Some of Margaret's color faded. "She was very angry with me."

"With good reason, no doubt."

Her chin came up. "I did not think so. And I must tell

you, Sir Justin, that I *still* refuse to marry you. I will stay here until you are better, but then—"

"*You* refuse to marry *me*?"

She looked confused. "Yes. That is why I ran away. But you know that. Mama said I must, and I . . . I *won't*."

Keighley was silent for a moment, frowning, then his mouth hardened. "I don't suppose you're joking? No, I can see you are not. Miss Mayfield, your mother is a scheming, shameless woman."

She stared at him.

"Let me inform you," he added, "that *I* absolutely refused to marry *you* when taxed with the obligation."

"You . . . but . . ."

"Precisely. And I was told that you had run away from home because of that refusal, because I would not have you."

Margaret sprang to her feet, scarlet with rage and embarrassment. "What?"

"I promise you it is true." He frowned again. "Let us begin at the beginning. There is a great deal I do not understand. As far as I recollect, I met you for the first time at your parents' dinner party. Had we met previously in London? I am abominably forgetful."

"No," answered Margaret curtly.

"Indeed. So we did not speak until I suggested a stroll in the garden, to which you, at least tacitly, agreed."

She started to protest then noticed that the conversation appeared to be tiring him. His face was paler, and his hand shook a little on the counterpane. "Should we talk now?" she wondered aloud. "You are still very ill."

"Thank you, but I should prefer to understand. And I am perfectly capable of speaking. We walked in the garden then, and I attempted a few polite remarks, to which you failed to respond. And then, for no reason I could discern, you appeared to run mad, clawing my coat and flinging yourself over a table to end unconscious on the ground. When I went to see what could be the matter, your parents came up and accused me of assault. Could you, Miss Mayfield, explain your behavior to me?"

His sarcasm made Margaret forget her scruples about his health, but it was still difficult to tell him what she had thought that night. She saw now that she had been mistaken. "I . . . I thought you were taking me to the summerhouse," she murmured, looking at the floor. "My father had locked it up because . . . because there had been . . ."

"The usual escapades in a summerhouse," finished Keighley. "I see. And what led you to imagine I would do such an idiotic thing? I am not famed for my polished manners, but I do retain certain remnants of decency."

Margaret wondered how to explain that she had been given such a derogatory picture of him that she expected any evil. "I . . . I had been given to understand," she stammered, "that . . . that you were not a proper person for me to know."

"Ah. Your mama again, I suppose?" She did not respond, but he nodded slightly. "I should have seen that. She has never missed an opportunity to criticize me elsewhere. So you expected me to be a blackguard? Perhaps you still do?"

Margaret wanted to say that the way he spoke to her did not suggest anything better, but she held her tongue because of his wound.

"And then your half-witted parents insisted you were compromised, as you were *not*, and that we must marry. Sensibly we both refused. However, you were not told that *I* had, and I was not told your views. Instead I was neatly maneuvered into chasing after you—and received a ball in the shoulder for my pains. You know, your mother should be the MP. I daresay she would be Prime Minister by this time."

"Well, I do not see why you came. I was perfectly all right."

"Indeed? And where did you think you were going?"

"To . . . Penzance."

"And?"

"What do you mean?"

"What did you expect to do there?" he added impatiently. Margaret was silent.

"I see. Well, you must go back home, of course. Your mother can no doubt fabricate some excuse for your absence. And I—"

"I *can't*," exclaimed the girl. The thought of returning home in disgrace was harrowing. "You need help."

"I shall get along. I have done so for a number of years without your assistance."

"But they said you require nursing, and I was going to—"

"I have not compromised you up to now," interrupted Keighley, "but if we stay together at this inn for any period of time, I would be hard put to defend myself from the accusation. And in any case, I do not want you here. I will send for someone to nurse me."

Margaret rose. "Certainly. I shall be more than glad to leave. I was only staying to make up for shooting you." But I won't go home, she thought. I'll go on to Penzance.

A thin smile curved his lips. "What did you find to tell the innkeeper? I wonder. Or have you left that to me?"

"I told him you were my brother." A thought occurred to her. "Oh, and I said your name was Harry Camden. I . . . I didn't want . . ."

"Very resourceful. Should it get back to the squire's son, I daresay he will be pleased with the imputation that he was shot by an unknown female."

"I said highwaymen did it. And that they stole our

luggage. Harry won't hear. The Camdens are quite a distance off. I couldn't think of another name in a hurry."

"Couldn't you? You have alarming lapses of intelligence, do you not?"

"I did my best!"

"God help us. And I suppose you do not see that your clumsy fabrication traps you here?"

"What do you mean?"

"Is my sister likely to abandon me to my valet, whom I meant to summon? That would cause enough talk to spread the story far beyond this place, whatever it is. And if you stay, I cannot send for anyone else, for I do not want to be recognized here with you. Can you really be so simple as not to see all this?" He frowned up at her with an effort, clearly at the end of his spurt of energy. "Or was this whole thing a plot to entrap me? I warn you it won't work."

"*Entrap* you? I wouldn't have you if you begged on your knees."

"Good. Because I won't be caught so, my girl. I shall marry at my own choice, and it won't be a wide-eyed schoolroom chit."

"I pity the woman you *do* chose." And with these words, Margaret stormed out of the room. Let him nurse himself, the odious man. He was every bit as bad as her mother had told her.

6

Margaret was down by the seawall before she calmed enough to marvel at her own behavior. She had argued heatedly with a near stranger, a man whom, only two days ago, she had thought she feared. And she never argued with anyone. What had come over her? It had happened almost automatically; she had not thought, she had simply reacted. But what was it about Justin Keighley that made her do so? He no longer terrified her, but somehow he roused emotions stronger than she had ever experienced and prompted behavior completely unlike her previous pattern. How could he? And why?

She sat down on the wall and gazed out over the water. It didn't make sense. One's character could not change overnight, could it? Margaret had always accepted others', particularly her mother's, opinion of her. She thought of herself as a quiet, unassuming girl of no more than average gifts. Now, suddenly, it was as if the person she knew were being swept away, and she was not at all certain she liked the feeling or the new Margaret who seemed to be emerging. She sighed. One thing, at least, was unquestionably true: she disliked Sir Justin Keighley intensely and bitterly resented his intrusion into her life.

"Excuse me, miss?" said a tentative young voice.

Margaret looked around to find a boy of twelve or thirteen standing before her, his cloth cap in his hands. "Yes?"

"Ma said you came down here. I'm to fetch you. The doctor's just come."

"Oh." She rose.

"We'd 'ave been back sooner, but he was out when I got to his house."

"Did *you* go?" asked Margaret wonderingly. The boy did not seem old enough to be sent such a distance alone.

"Yes, miss. I be Jem Appleby, you know."

"Mrs. Appleby's son, yes. She told me she was sending you. But I didn't know you were so young."

"I'm thirteen! In two years I shall go to sea with the fishing boats, like my brother Bob."

"But what about your schooling?"

Jem looked disdainful. "I've finished with school. I can read and write a treat, I can."

Margaret gazed at him; though she had sometimes chatted with her maid, who probably came from a family like Jem's, they had never talked of the other girl's life. Jem Appleby was a new type for Margaret. "Do you want to go to sea?" she asked.

The boy raised incredulous blue eyes to hers. "Course I do. Who wouldn't?"

"I wouldn't."

"Oh, girls." He shrugged.

Smiling a little, Margaret watched him as they walked back up the hill to the Red Lion. Jem was a small lad, but wiry and work-toughened. He had curly brown hair, round red cheeks, and a snub nose, and his clothes, though well-kept by his mother, showed the effects of hard usage. "What do you do now?" she asked him. "Do you help at the inn?"

He nodded without much enthusiasm. "I see to the horses."

"You don't care for that?"

"Nah. They're stupid beasts. Are we to stop for old Mrs. Dowling? Ma told me to ask."

With a start, Margaret remembered their errand. "Oh, yes, I suppose we should. The doctor will want to speak to her. Where is . . ."

"There," replied Jem smugly, pointing to a cottage just up the hill from where they stood. "I came this way on purpose."

"Very clever. You are a good navigator."

He grinned, showing a generous mouthful of white teeth. "You should see me on the water. When I can get out, anyway."

"Do you have a boat?" queried Margaret, surprised.

Before answering, Jem cupped his hands around his mouth and shouted, "Mrs. Dowling, Doctor's come." Then he turned back and said, "It's not much. A dinghy. But I've rigged her up with a sail and all. She runs before the wind well enough."

"I should like to see it. Does it have a name?"

"*She's* the *Gull*," he replied, partly instructing, partly pleased by her interest. "Perhaps I'll take you—"

"A fine way to go on," interrupted Mrs. Dowling, appearing in the doorway of her cottage. "Shouting in the street instead of knocking like a civilized person. I'll be telling your mother of this, young Jemmy."

Jem shrugged and grimaced. "Doctor's come," he said again.

"Aye. I heard you. So did everyone else in the village, I'll be bound. Are we waiting for them?"

"Nah." Jem ducked his head and hurried up the hill toward the tavern. Margaret followed more slowly with Mrs. Dowling.

"That's a pesky lad," complained the latter. "Mad for

the sea. Reckon he'll be drowned, like so many of 'em are."

"Don't say that."

Mrs. Dowling peered up at her from under her bushy white brows. "Do you fear bad luck? Nay, I know better than that. But the sea takes most of our men hereabouts."

Margaret stole a look over her shoulder. The water below was calm, but she could not restrain a small shiver of apprehension. Why did Jem Appleby want to join the fishing fleets? A job in his father's inn seemed much pleasanter to her.

Mrs. Appleby met them at the door of the Red Lion. "Doctor's upstairs with him now," she said. "I told him you'd be right along, miss."

"Thank you. I . . . Did you notice if my brother was . . ."

"He's gone off again." The woman smiled a little. "I suppose your quarrel tired him out." When Margaret looked stricken, she added, "Brothers and sisters always quarrel, miss. It can't have hurt him any." She exchanged a look with Mrs. Dowling that Margaret probably would have found comforting if she had been paying any heed, but she was already at the foot of the stairs and starting up.

"There." Mrs. Appleby addressed Mrs. Dowling when Margaret had disappeared. "I told you they were all right. If you could have heard them going at it this morning."

"Over what?"

"I couldn't tell that. I don't listen at keyholes. But they were scrapping like they'd done it all their lives."

"Humph," answered Mrs. Dowling, starting slowly up the stairs.

The doctor was not what Margaret had expected. Her own family practitioner was a jovial, white-haired gentleman she had known as long as she could remember, but the Falmouth doctor was a young man, dressed very fashionably, with a haughty manner.

"Are you the sister?" he asked when Margaret came in.

She nodded. "How is he?" She could see that Keighley had lapsed into unconsciousness again since their talk, and from the look of him, the exchange had exhausted all his meager resources.

"Not good," replied the doctor. "The wound is not serious in itself, but he is very weak. He must have lost quite a bit of blood."

His tone was so critical that Margaret started to apologize, but she was forestalled by Mrs. Dowling's voice from the door. "Aye, that he did," she agreed. "They had a time getting him down here from the road."

"Who are you?" inquired the man coldly, looking Mrs. Dowling up and down.

"Th-This is Mrs. Dowling," stammered Margaret. "She was kind enough to treat my brother. She took out the bullet. Mrs. Dowling, this is Dr. . . ."

"Brice," he finished. "You removed the ball from his shoulder?"

Mrs. Dowling nodded, a wicked grin on her wrinkled face.

Dr. Brice closed his black bag with a snap. "I don't see what there is for me to do in that case," he added.

"B—But can you not look at him?" asked Margaret. "Tell me if I am doing the right things? I am very worried."

Slightly mollified, the doctor turned a shoulder to Mrs. Dowling and answered, "I have examined him. He is weak, as I said. He needs rest and, as soon as possible, sustaining soups and whatever food he can take. If there is no infection, he should recover in a few weeks. He seems a strong specimen."

"How can I keep off infection?" asked Margaret.

He shrugged. "Keep the wound clean. Do not allow him to strain it in any way." Mrs. Dowling chuckled, and he stiffened alarmingly. "I must go. It is a *very* long ride to Falmouth." His tone implied that he had made it for nothing.

"But . . ." began Margaret.

"I have many calls on my time," he added.

Meeting his rather hard brown eyes, she nodded. "I see. What do we owe you?"

"One guinea."

"*What?*" screeched Mrs. Dowling. "For what? You didn't do nothing."

The doctor fixed her with an icy gaze. "I am a London-trained physician . . . madam. And I rode more than an hour to get here. The fee is moderate, considering."

"It's barefaced robbery," retorted Mrs. Dowling. "The gentleman's already been *shot* by highwaymen."

"Please," protested Margaret, who had fetched the money by this time. She handed it to the doctor. "Thank you for coming." Mrs. Dowling, outraged, was about to speak again, but Margaret waved her to silence. Dr. Brice bowed coldly and strode out.

"Young jackass," muttered the midwife. "I've seen his like time and again. Think they know everything when they can hardly birth a baby without the mother doing all the work."

Privately Margaret agreed with her. Dr. Brice had been singularly unhelpful. But she did not want to fall into a long discussion of his shortcomings. "How does my brother look to you?" she asked. "He was awake for a while this morning, but now . . ."

"Aye. When you quarreled," agreed Mrs. Dowling. At Margaret's wince, she added, "It won't have done him any harm, miss. It's good for men to quarrel—keeps them occupied. It's not unnatural for a wounded man to wake and then go off again. It may happen more than once."

"I see." Margaret watched as Mrs. Dowling examined Keighley.

"He's a bit better, I think. You should get something inside him as soon as may be. Flossie Appleby will have some broth on."

"I'll get a bowl."

"No use till he wakes again, but give him some then. I'll come by tomorrow, if you like."

"Please do."

The midwife nodded and turned away. Margaret heard her slow steps descending the stairs as she sat down in the armchair by the window once again. No matter what they said, she felt a little guilty for having quarreled with Keighley. However exasperating the man was, he was also wounded and weak. She should have humored him. But when she thought again of some of the things he had said to her, her fists clenched. One couldn't ignore such remarks. In the future she would simply have to keep their conversations off personal matters. They could talk about the weather or politics, but not about themselves. Picking up some sewing she had laid aside hours ago, one of her garments that had been badly torn while lying in the road, she settled down to a quiet afternoon, putting her dispute with Sir Justin firmly from her mind.

The patient did not wake again that day. But his breathing sounded more like sleep than before, and Margaret was not seriously worried. At dinnertime she was relieved by Annie Appleby, and went downstairs to eat. Afterward she strolled outside and down the twisting lane to the shore. The sun was setting behind the cliff, throwing long, thin shadows across the golden sea, and there was a soft breeze scented with blossoms. Margaret walked along the seawall again, in the opposite direction from yesterday, and enjoyed the calm beauty of the scene. She noticed a small boat out on the water, with a single triangular sail and one lone occupant. Leaning on the wall to watch for a moment, she realized the sailor was Jem Appleby, and she waved to him. He responded briefly, then turned back to the management of his sail and tiller. He was headed for the mouth of the shallow bay on which the village stood. Margaret followed the progress of the tiny craft for several minutes—Jem appeared to be having a fine time as it dipped and wobbled in the waves—then she went on until she had reached the end of the village houses. Here, where the road curved back inland, there were steps set into the wall leading down to the beach. Glancing over her shoulder, Margaret saw that there was at least a half hour of light left, so she descended and continued her walk along the sand. The stony cliff rose to her right, and the waves murmured on the other side. A flowering vine that she did not recognize spilled orange blossoms over the rocks above her head. All in all, it was a beautiful place, and she dawdled a bit looking at it.

Coming around an outcropping of stone, she discovered that the village bay was not the only one nearby. Here was a much smaller indentation, hardly thirty feet across but very deeply cut into the cliff and into the sea bottom. Everything was in shadow now, but she turned to walk along it anyway, for she could hear the sound of a stream from the back.

There were more growing things in this sheltered spot, and as she pushed through a row of bushes Margaret found what she sought. A trickle of water, too slight to be called a fall, wet the cliff and fell into a rock pool above the level of the sea. It was surrounded by moss and overhung by one slender tree and the vine she had seen before. It seemed the loveliest place Margaret had ever seen. She knelt, oblivious of her gown, and gazed into the clear water. Her wavering reflection there showed an unfamiliar smile of delight, and she realized that she had never before gone exploring alone and found a secret spot. She took a deep breath, savoring the bouquet of scents around her. She felt wonderful.

Margaret lingered by the pool until it was nearly dark and left it reluctantly even then. But she told herself she would come back every day, without fail. At the Red Lion all was well, and she prepared for bed in a much better humor than she had last night. Her situation was still far from satisfactory, but somehow she minded it less. Something seemed to be happening to her. She had thought this morning that the change was unfortunate, but now she was no longer sure. If the new Margaret had evenings like this one, she might be a person well worth knowing after all.

7

Several days passed peacefully. Sir Justin slept most of the time, waking only briefly to eat or sometimes murmur a few sentences. At first Margaret feared that he had taken a fever, but Mrs. Dowling assured her that he was merely weak and would soon recover more fully. In the meantime, he did not require constant watching. If someone was within call, as they always were at the small tavern, it was enough. Thus Margaret found herself with a good deal of unoccupied time. She sat with Keighley part of the day, but she also walked, always stopping at her newfound hideaway, and often going on more than two miles along the shore.

She had been a sedentary girl, but here there were no books to read and no mother to find indoor tasks for her. Her usually negligible appetite improved with the exercise and with Mrs. Appleby's good, simple food, as did her color. By the end of her first week in the village, Margaret's cheeks were redder than they had ever been, and her figure more rounded. Indeed, her mother might have looked twice before she recognized her overthin, pale, withdrawn daughter in this carefree, bright-eyed young woman. With no immediate worries, Margaret discovered a new pleasure in the present. Sometime she would have to make decisions, but for now she felt unfettered and surprisingly pleased with herself.

This idyllic mood was broken at the beginning of the second week. When she entered Keighley's bedchamber that morning, she found him fully conscious again, propped up on pillows, and not in the best of humors. "So, you *are* still here," he said when she came in. "I thought perhaps you had left me to the care of our rustic hosts' daughter."

"Annie offered to sit with you at night," she replied. "She has nursed before. She is very skillful."

Keighley shrugged, then winced at the pain in his shoulder. "And you continue to play the ministering sister, I suppose?" he added irritably. "What a ridiculous farce."

Hoping to avoid a dispute, Margaret said nothing.

But her silence merely goaded him further. "What is the date?" he snapped. And when she told him, he cursed.

"We have had a doctor," she added soothingly. "He said you will be all right after a . . . while."

"*Weeks*," responded Keighley savagely. "I know more than you do about gunshot wounds. I feel weak as a blasted kitten, and I shan't be able to ride for at least two weeks. You spare no pains when you meddle in a man's life."

Against her best resolves, Margaret began to be angry. "I? I didn't meddle. It was you who did that. Why didn't you simply let me escape from home, as I wished to?"

This question was too close to Sir Justin's own opinion to contest. But the truth of her point merely made him angrier at her. "We needn't go over that again," he replied bitingly. "What are we to do *now?*"

Margaret looked at him. "Do?"

"Do?" he echoed, in a savagely mocking tone. "Must you repeat my words in that witless way?"

She clenched her fists at her side and strove to remember that this man was hurt. Probably his wound was paining him even now. She must try to control her temper, though all she wanted was to give him the sharpest setdown he had ever received in his life. "I did so," she said carefully, "because I did not understand what you meant. I do not see that there is anything to be done until you are better."

"Do you not?" His tone remained bitterly sarcastic. "In other words, I am to lie here flat on my back and go slowly mad from boredom while you . . ." He paused and surveyed her. "What *have* you been doing? You look . . . better."

This was hardly complimentary, but it was less inflaming. "There is little to do in this village," admitted Margaret. "I have walked on the beach a good deal."

"I see. Well, I can't do *that*, thanks to you."

"To yourself," she retorted, then hurriedly added, "There are some cards. I found them last night. Or we might talk. I know it is fatiguing to lie in bed all day. When I had a fever three years—"

"Talk to *you?* I should be more amused staring at the ceiling. And I doubt you play cards any better than you converse. In my worse nightmares I never imagined being stranded in the middle of nowhere with a half-witted schoolgirl."

The rags of Margaret's temper deserted her. The fact that Keighley was wounded, and irritable because of it, fled from her mind. She saw only that he was the most arrogant, unpleasant, dislikable man on earth. "*Stare* at the ceiling, then," she cried. "I don't care. I didn't want you here. I didn't want ever to see you again after that dreadful dinner party. Amuse *yourself*. I shan't give the matter another thought." And she turned and fled the room.

Left alone, Justin Keighley did gaze pensively at the

smooth white plaster above his bed. But what he saw was a pair of flashing blue eyes and a glowing, animated face surrounded by pale gold curls. Perhaps he had been wrong about the Mayfield chit. Though clearly not very intelligent, she did have some spirit after all. He sighed. He supposed he would have to be at least polite to her, and perhaps even endure a hand or two of cards, for she was his only source of amusement in this damnable situation, and he had always been distressingly prone to boredom. He sighed again, wondering if he should call her back. But it was too late and, besides, he had not come to *that* yet. She would be back and then he would . . . not apologize but exert some part of his not inconsiderable charm, enough to squeeze whatever diversion he could from an unpromising subject.

Margaret had stormed down the stairs and out of the house into the July sunshine. She was so incensed that she strode right by the passage leading down to the sea, instead going along the road on the clifftop. She realized her mistake when she came to the point where this lane branched to join the main road on the left and to become a twisting village street on the other side. She took the latter; she would get to the beach the long way.

Her temper was cooling. She was able now to shake her head at the strangeness of her plight. That she, Margaret Mayfield, should spend her days in noisy argument with Sir Justin Keighley was so unexpected, and astonishing, that she could hardly take it in. She thought of various acquaintances and what they would say if they knew and, unwillingly, a smile began to curve her lips.

How her friends would gape. And her parents—they would flatly refuse to believe it. When she imagined their stunned faces, Margaret laughed aloud.

"I'm glad to see ye so merry," said a voice above her head. "Your brother must be better, then."

Startled, Margaret looked up. Her path had wound

through the village to a point she recognized, and Mrs. Dowling leaned out of her cottage window overhead. "Tell the joke," added the old woman. "I could use a laugh this morning, and no mistake."

"There's no joke," replied Margaret. "I was just . . ." And with this, she realized what she *had* been doing—laughing at her parents—and was silenced.

"Well, well," said Mrs. Dowling. "Wait a minute, and I'll come down and let you in."

"Oh, no, I'm going to the beach," answered Margaret, but Mrs. Dowling was already gone. She could hear the door latch being lifted. Margaret stirred uneasily. She had not quite gotten over her first reaction to Mrs. Dowling, despite the old woman's help and patent goodwill. Every time she saw her, she was irresistibly reminded of a witch, and she could not shake off the notion that there was something sinister about her, though she had told herself a hundred times that this was silly.

"Come in, come in," urged Mrs. Dowling, holding her door open insistently. Margaret tried to make some excuse, but it was brushed aside, and she found herself in the cottage, being ushered through a narrow hall to the back of the building. "We'll sit outside," added her hostess. "It bain't hot yet."

She opened another door at the rear of the house and waved Margaret through. At the threshold the girl paused and drew in a startled breath. Mrs. Dowling's simple cottage was graced with a tiny terrace at the back, a simple flagged square bordered by a low stone wall on three sides. Flowering shrubs in pots sat on this wall, and the ocean spread out far below in a gorgeous panorama. It was the last sort of place she would have expected to find here, and she turned to look at the old woman with new eyes.

"This is where I hang my laundry," said the latter complacently as she followed Margaret out. "And we used to sit here of an evening, Bob and me, afore he died."

"Y—Your husband?"

She nodded. "And a good one, too. He was lost off a fishing boat in 'ninety-nine. He liked this place, he did." She looked around the terrace. "Took care of the flowers."

Fascinated, Margaret followed her glance, all her ideas about Mrs. Dowling undergoing hurried revision. "It's lovely."

"It is that." Mrs. Dowling moved to the wall and sat down next to a bush of scarlet blossoms. She patted the stone next to her. "Sit here, dearie. I've som'at to say to you."

Surprised, Margaret obeyed.

Her hostess did not speak at once, but rather looked out to sea as if she had forgotten her request. Finally she said, "Men be odd creatures. Very odd."

Margaret stared at her, and Mrs. Dowling turned slightly and met her eyes. "They don't think like us," she continued. "They get a maggot in their heads and run mad over a thing that any woman would shrug off in an instant. *How* I used to laugh at my Bob—when he wasn't looking, of course—and how we used to brangle about some of his odd notions."

"D-Did you?" Margaret was at a loss.

"That we did." Mrs. Dowling grinned, and Margaret had a sudden vision of a much younger woman with wicked, dancing eyes. "And how we made up for it afterward!"

Margaret's eyes grew wider. No one had ever spoken to her like this about men, certainly not her mother. Indeed, she had formed very few opinions about the sex beyond the stark division between good and bad inculcated very early. But Mrs. Dowling's remarks and tone seemed to imply that there was a great deal more to know, and Margaret found herself intrigued. "Your husband was a fisherman?" she asked, trying to encourage the woman to go on without seeming too eager.

Mrs. Dowling merely nodded, and the girl could not immediately think of another question. A silence fell between them, which lengthened until Margaret felt uneasy. Some of her old shyness returned, and she could think of no remark to end the pause. She was about to rise and admire one of the shrubs when Mrs. Dowling said abruptly, "Mayhap the man *is* your brother. Flos Appleby thinks so, and she sees more of you than me. But if he bain't . . ." She paused and gazed into Margaret's face, as if to find the truth there. Margaret, who had started inwardly when she first spoke, strove to remain impassive. Mrs. Dowling shrugged. "If he bain't," she went on, "he's worth the candle. That's all I meant to say."

"Worth . . ." The girl frowned.

"I've seen a deal of people in my time. And mostly men and women together, bringing babies into the world. I know a fine specimen of a man when I see one."

Now Margaret did rise. She walked to the corner of the terrace and looked down over the sea, struggling with herself. Part of her wanted to protest hotly and tell Mrs. Dowling exactly what a despicable person Justin Keighley was. But another part kept her silent and finally forced out the words, "I'm sure my brother would be very flattered by your opinion."

"Aye. Well, you know best, miss. Flos Appleby says you and the gentleman quarrel whenever he's awake. She takes that to mean you are brother and sister." She laughed. "Flos *would* think that; she and Dan get on like they grew up together. But I know better. Bob and me fought like cats, but we always ended up somewheres else before we was done."

Margaret did not understand precisely what the old woman meant, but she caught enough to realize that she was implying some romantic connection between herself and Keighley. "I assure you, you are mistaken," she replied earnestly. "There is nothing like *that* involved." By not mentioning the false "brother" story, she was able to speak with absolute conviction.

Mrs. Dowling eyed her, looking both puzzled and curious.

"I should get back to my . . . my brother now," added Margaret. "Thank you for asking me in."

In another moment she was walking back toward the inn after a hasty farewell. As she went she frowned. Had Mrs. Dowling believed her denials? It would ruin everything if the old woman began telling the villagers that Margaret and Keighley were not brother and sister. She would have to visit her again and make sure she did not. When she decided this, Margaret at once felt better. She hadn't the least notion that this was partly because she was curious to hear more on the subject of men and their oddness.

Sir Justin was finishing a bowl of broth from a tray across his knees when Margaret came in. He greeted her much more cordially than she had expected and asked her to sit down. He had indeed been bored through his first morning of full wakefulness, and he was ready to embrace any form of amusement. For her part, Margaret a little regretted her show of temper and was ready to do what she could for her patient.

"Have you had luncheon?" Keighley asked politely. "I believe Mrs. Appleby mentioned a lamb pie."

"I never eat at midday." This was not strictly true. She never had because she had never been hungry at this time, but recently she sometimes ate the luncheon the landlady pressed on her when she returned from one of her walks. However, she did not think it was Keighley's place to be urging food on her. She wished to be cordial to him but not to appear subject to his guidance in any way. "Have you finished?" she added, indicating the now empty bowl.

"Yes."

She leaned over him and took the tray, carrying it to a small table in the hall outside, where one of the Appleby girls would find it.

"Have you plans for the afternoon?" Sir Justin called after her, in a tone more eager and conciliatory than any she had heard him use.

"No," she replied, coming back into the room. "Can I do something for you?" As she said this she felt a strange impulse to giggle. They were talking to each other as carefully as her mother did to Mrs. Kane, her only rival for "great lady" of their neighborhood in Devon and, consequently, her deadliest enemy.

"It is very slow, lying here. It appears they have no books at this inn. You mentioned cards. I thought we might try a hand, if you are still willing."

"Of course. I'll fetch them." Turning away, Margaret hid a smile. The insufferable Sir Justin Keighley had certainly altered since the morning. A few hours' boredom was apparently salutary. She found the cards and ran lightly back upstairs, still smiling. There was a certain pleasure in this change. He deserved a bit of chastening.

"Do you play piquet?" Keighley asked when she presented the deck.

Margaret shook her head.

"Whist? Bezique?"

"I fear I've rarely played cards. The only game I know is Patience." For an instant his face showed such chagrin that Margaret had to suppress another giggle. "I am willing to learn," she added with a sweet smile.

Justin closed his eyes briefly, then opened them with a sigh. If he had had to describe his idea of hell, it probably would have closely resembled his present situation. No doubt the girl would be an execrable cardplayer. Perhaps even boredom was preferable to trying to teach her a game. He considered this alternative but rejected it. "Is that tray still about?" he asked. "We can put it here and use it for a table."

Margaret brought the wooden tray back, after removing the dishes, and placed it at his side on the coverlet.

"All right," he continued wearily, fanning the deck out on it with his good hand. "We will try piquet, I think. These are the rules."

An hour later, Margaret hunched, frowning, over the cards in her hand while Sir Justin gazed at her with a look of such rigidly controlled fury that Mrs. Dowling might have been alarmed at her patient's state. "Are you going to play?" he asked. His tone would have withered any number of habitués of White's, where Keighley was known as one of the finest cardplayers in London.

But Margaret was concentrating too closely to notice. She had been making an intense effort in the past hour to remember all the rules he had thrown at her and to play a creditable game. This seemed to become ever more difficult as time passed, and at the moment she was completely at a loss. "Do you think," she responded without looking up, "that all the cards are here? I have not seen the jack of hearts. Have you had it?"

Sir Justin clenched his teeth, and his face reddened ominously. "Did you not count the deck before we began?" he said slowly, enunciating each word as if he feared to let it out.

"I didn't think to. I should have. I daresay these cards have been lying about for years."

"You are the stupidest girl I have ever had the misfortune to encounter!" exploded her companion. "Not only are you utterly unable to grasp the simplest set of rules, but you don't even have the sense to examine cards before you begin a game. Even an idiot does that much."

"Indeed?" Margaret's chin had come up in outrage. "Why didn't you do it, then? *You* are supposed to be the expert. I never claimed to know anything of cards."

"I *assumed* you had taken care of the matter," he snapped venomously. But her point was so telling that he abandoned this line and added, "In any case, I think we may dispense with cards. You will never be even an average player."

"I don't think that is fair. I have scarcely tried." Margaret did not understand the rage of a first-rate player after an hour of hesitations and mistakes, and thus she failed to comprehend the depth of his emotion.

"*Do* try the next time, then. Perhaps if you strain your faculties to the utmost, you can at least learn the rules."

"Well, you are a very poor teacher. You did not explain them at all clearly. My governess used to—"

Keighley seemed to swell with rage. "I could not be *less* interested in what your governess used to do. Nor in your opinion of my teaching abilities. Let us simply abandon this effort, for our *mutual* benefit."

Margaret stared at him. "Very well. I do not see why you are so angry. It is only a card game, after all."

As he struggled to form a reply to this astonishingly naive statement, Sir Justin had a sudden vision of his circle at White's. What would Denison or, better, Rowley, do faced with this girl's attitude? The answer was so ludicrous that much of his anger dissipated. He almost wished he could set Margaret down among them and watch their faces as she wondered why they became so heated over "only a card game."

"Shall we do something else?" the girl was inquiring blithely. "Or are you tired out?"

Keighley sank back on his pillows with a sigh and a short laugh. "What would you suggest?"

"It *is* difficult. There is little to do indoors here. We could just talk, I suppose." She sounded a bit doubtful.

He was even more so. "About what?"

Margaret remembered one of her earlier ideas. "Politics, perhaps. You are very interested in political matters, I know, and I . . ."

"And you are as ignorant about them as about piquet," he finished.

"I am *not*. I have listened to political discussions all my life."

"I would hardly call your father's complacent self-congratulations political discussions."

"How dare you? He is a highly respected Member of Parliament and . . ."

"And a pompous fool."

Margaret sprang to her feet, her fists clenched at her sides. "Why, why you . . ."

Keighley gazed appreciatively at her glowing cheeks and flashing blue eyes. This was much more amusing than trying to teach the chit cards. "All right, then," he challenged. "What do you know about the Corn Laws?"

Margaret struggled with herself. She wanted to give him a blistering setdown or leave him alone again to amuse himself, but the amused look on his face suggested that he was waiting for her to do either of those things, and to laugh at her for it. It would be far better to show him that she knew as much as he—or more.

"The Corn Laws," she began icily, "are to aid agriculture by stopping the import of cheap foreign wheat. The landowners were being ground down and required protection. And the poor should realize that a good price for wheat is necessary so that—"

"So that they may starve," he interrupted. But despite his sarcasm, he appeared a bit surprised. "People can't pay a good price if they have nothing, which is what we are leaving our laborers these days. In any case, the law failed even to do what it promised."

"If they were willing to work hard," began Margaret.

"Work?" Keighley shook his head. "What do you know of work? Have you ever bent in the fields or been shut in a dark factory for sixteen hours, and for a sum that would not purchase the buttons on that gown? And those are the *lucky* ones. Many don't even have work. There is no work for them."

His vehemence confused Margaret. Her father had never talked of these issues in such an impassioned tone, nor had Philip. Nonetheless, she ventured. "A great many men have made fortunes in trade. There are opportunities . . ."

"Oh, stop this. You haven't any idea what you are talking about. You have never seen a truly poor man in your life. You are just like all of Society, blind to the realities that surround you. You live in London without the least glance into the noisome slums that abound there. It was the same in Brussels during the war. They held balls—*balls*—while men were fighting and dying not five miles distant. And in London one hardly knew a war was going on. Despicable! But it is unlikely to last much longer, I can tell you. If the so-called ruling class does not allow some reforms soon, it will be overwhelmed by what lies beneath."

Margaret gazed at him, silenced. Whatever she might think of his opinions, his vehemence had impressed her. It was obvious that these ideas were extremely important to him. She had not thought him capable of such serious feelings.

Seeing her astonished expression, Keighley laughed harshly. "I see you share everyone else's opinion of my beliefs," he added. "My aunt, my grandmother, most of my former friends, even my political allies find me far too radical. Why can people not see the inevitable?"

Margaret had no answer to this or, indeed, to any of his statements. But before her silence could grow noticeable, they were interrupted by a brisk knock on the open door and the entrance of Jemmy Appleby, carrying a gigantic, glistening fish. "Ma says to ask if you'll have this for dinner," he said, dangling the creature by its tail before them. "I caught it myself, just now," he added proudly.

Margaret stared at the silvery scales, only inches from her eyes, with awe. The fish's round, dead eye returned her gaze. And suddenly, without warning, Justin Keighley began to laugh.

He laughed until he had to put a hand to his shoulder to ease the pain, until tears ran down his cheeks, until Margaret and Jemmy frowned at him in perplexity. And when he finally brought himself under control again, he was worn out with laughter and had to sink back on his pillows in exhaustion.

"Won't it do?" asked Jemmy uneasily. "It's a fine one, a flounder. Ma said she'd bake it nice."

Keighley started to laugh again, more weakly.

"It will do very well," answered Margaret, seeing Sir Justin's tiredness. "Come, let us go and tell your mother so." Putting a hand on Jemmy's shoulder, she guided him out of the room. "I will be back at dinnertime," she said to Keighley, who simply nodded.

But as she walked down the stairs she puzzled over the new facets of his personality she had seen today. She would never have predicted the passionate interest he had shown in the poor, and his hearty laughter had been still more surprising. She recalled his face as he laughed. It had been nothing like the Keighley she had been told about and thought she had met. Indeed, she could not reconcile that burst of humor with anything she knew about the man. It was exceedingly odd.

With this thought, Mrs. Dowling's words recurred to her. Apparently the old woman was right. Men were odd, very odd. Margaret felt another flash of the curiosity those words had engendered. She would see Mrs. Dowling again soon.

8

Sir Justin napped through the late afternoon, worn out by his earlier exertions. But when dinnertime came, he roused and flatly refused to remain in bed for the meal. He *would* get up, he insisted, and he would even come downstairs and eat at table like a civilized man. Margaret, Annie, and Mrs. Appleby argued with him, but he was adamant, and finally Mr. Appleby was summoned to help him dress and come down.

Margaret waited anxiously at the foot of the stairs and followed the pair into the parlor, where a table had been set for them. Keighley was leaning heavily on the innkeeper, and she still thought he was making a mistake. He sighed when he was settled in his chair. "Weak as a kitten." He leaned back. "Blast it."

"You should stay in bed for . . ." began Margaret.

"Please. Spare me. We have been through all that. Let us talk instead of coats. I have, of course, only my riding coat with me. With one shirt, and so on. Is there any place in this village where I may add to that store?"

Margaret shook her head. "It is a very small place. There aren't any shops except the greengrocer and . . ."

"I see." He surveyed her blue cambric gown. "You at least have a change of clothes, I suppose?"

"Yes. I brought three dresses with me."

"Yes." He sighed again. "Well, I shall have to ask Appleby to send someone to the nearest town."

"Jemmy will go."

"That boy with the fish?" Keighley smiled slightly.

"Yes. He does all the errands. He is very resourceful."

"Somehow that does not surprise me."

At this moment Jemmy himself entered the room, weighed down by a large platter upon which rested his fish—baked and garnished and looking splendid. "Ma said I could bring it," the boy informed them. "It looks prime, don't it?" Setting the platter in the center of the table, he eyed his catch complacently.

"It does," agreed Margaret.

"Did you get it in the bay?" asked Keighley.

" 'Bout a hundred yards beyond the mouth. I caught three, but this is the biggest."

"You must have a tight boat. The seas were high today."

"Aw, she's all right." Jemmy surveyed Sir Justin with a shrewd air. "*You* have a boat, I guess."

He smiled and nodded. "I keep her at Southampton."

The boy leaned forward eagerly. "Forty-footer, I'll bet."

"Not quite so big, but she's a neat little thing."

"I daresay." Jemmy proceeded to pelt Keighley with questions about his boat, its anchorage, and a great many other nautical matters. Margaret was lost almost immediately in a welter of sloops and ketches, gaff rigging, spars, sheets that did not seem to bear any relation to bed linen, and other terms she could not even begin to translate. When the rapid conversation finally slowed, the light of hero worship had appeared in Jemmy Appleby's eyes, and Keighley was looking both amused and kindly. "I'll show you my boat anytime you like," promised the boy. "She ain't much to look at, but she rides well for a dinghy."

"I should like to see her," agreed Keighley solemnly. "We shall have to wait until my arm is better. Then perhaps you can take me out."

"Yes, sir," replied Jemmy fervently.

"Now, however," interrupted Margaret, "we had better try this splendid fish, or it will be cold."

Jemmy started, just as his mother's voice was heard calling from the kitchen. "Lord, I've got to fetch the potatoes," he exclaimed, and ran for the corridor.

Keighley laughed, as did Margaret after a moment. He picked up the serving piece and said, "May I give you some of our friend's excellent catch?"

"Yes, indeed. He is a nice boy, isn't he?"

"Very engaging."

Jemmy brought the rest of the dishes at full speed. He showed some inclination to linger after the last, but his mother called him again, and he went reluctantly.

Margaret and Sir Justin ate in silence for a time. He was looking tired, and she hardly knew what topic to begin that would not cause friction. At last, however, she felt she must speak, so she said, "I have been thinking about what you said this morning."

He looked surprised. "Have you?"

"Yes. About the poor. I am very sorry for them, too, you know, and so is my father."

Keighley looked skeptical.

"He is! But the poor will not be helped if the landowning classes cannot sell their corn for a decent price. And their rioting and machinery breaking will do them no good. Indeed, it only makes people angry."

Her companion sat back with a sigh. For a moment it seemed that he would not reply, then he ran a hand over his eyes and said, "It certainly does that. But those people make no effort to understand the desperation behind the riots and protests."

"Yes, but . . . well, this very year there was that riot in London. They looted shops and burned a building."

"Their purpose was to present a petition of grievances to the Prince," said Sir Justin. "Surely an acceptable one."

"But—"

"But it got out of hand and turned to violence—yes. I cannot deny that. I would say, however, that such violence arises out of the frustration felt by those whose petitions are, at best, ignored. No one *listens* to them, you see."

Margaret pondered this. She knew how it felt to have one's opinions ignored, but she could not imagine setting fire to a mill or attacking a constable as a result. Her expression must have mirrored her thoughts, for Keighley added, "I realize you don't understand. So few do. It continually amazes me; it seems so obvious."

"Your own ideas are always obvious, seemingly," she replied, a bit piqued. Did he think he was invariably right? "Do *you* ever listen?"

He looked startled. "Actually, I do—quite often."

"But not to someone like me." She gazed at him. His hazel eyes met her blue ones with bemused puzzlement.

He sat back again and examined her carefully. Something had happened to the timorous, wearisome girl he had met at the Mayfields' dinner. That girl would never have spoken to him so or stared so challengingly. Indeed, he was not certain any woman had ever fixed his eye in just that way. "What have you been up to?" he asked. "You have changed all out of recognition."

Margaret's stare became perplexed, then her eyes dropped and some of her shyness returned. In her interest in the subject, and in Keighley's very unusual opinions, she had almost forgotten who he was and where they were and why.

"Can shooting me have brought out this new character?" he added, half teasingly. "If so, I hope it does not become fashionable."

She flushed, keeping her eyes on her plate.

"Please do not retreat into your tedious former persona. I'm not certain I could endure it."

A spark of anger made Margaret look up.

"That is better. Shall I insult you further? Will that make you speak?"

"You *are* a dreadful man."

"Aren't I?" he agreed cordially. "Perhaps you would prefer to insult me?"

"I should greatly prefer it, but I am too well bred to do so."

"Now where, Miss Mayfield, did you find that riposte? You must tell me. I would swear it was not in the head of the whining chit I met at your parents' home. Or are you the most skilled dissembler in the realm? I don't believe it. Something *has* happened to you."

Margaret considered him frowningly. What right had he to talk to her in this way? Yet she could not deny that he was right. She repeatedly astonished herself with the things she found to say, particularly to him, recently. Where did they come from? And what had happened to her? "I . . . I don't know," she stammered finally.

Keighley regarded her with more interest than he had shown, or indeed felt, in the whole course of their acquaintance. "Do you not?" he said meditatively. "I wonder."

A silence fell. Margaret eyed her companion nervously, but he seemed lost in thought.

"Tell me," he said finally, "when we were talking just now, why were you so eager? What were you thinking of?"

"I was interested in what you were saying."

"Yes?" he encouraged her when she stopped.

"That is all."

"But have you never been interested in what someone was saying before?"

"Well, of course I have, but . . ." Margaret paused. When her parents and Philip talked of the Corn Laws or other political issues, they never seemed as engrossing as when Keighley had spoken about them today. And it was the same when the Mayfields had political gatherings at the house. She had not, in fact, been interested in hearing them. She thought of other conversations—during the season or with her mother about household matters—and was astounded to realize that she had probably never been so caught up by a topic as she had been today. Why? She reexamined her memories. Philip and her parents made things so dull, and so did her mother's friends whom she had met in London. Usually she had shut off her mind after two or three exchanges, and since few ever addressed her, she had spent most of her social encounters in a kind of dream. Margaret blinked. Perhaps she had spent most of her *life* in a dream. This idea was so unsettling that she shivered.

"What is it?" asked Keighley, who had been watching her curiously.

"Nothing." She was not going to tell *him* these thoughts.

He gazed at her.

"Why do you talk as you do?"

"What?"

Margaret flushed again. "I mean, what made you believe as you do? You are so . . . so vehement in your opinions. Why?"

Keighley put his chin in his hand and frowned. Margaret followed each move. She was intensely interested in the answer to her questions, though she had not known this until she voiced them. From their first meeting, she had been puzzled and unsettled by Keighley's emotional effect on her. He had made her react in unaccustomed ways and with unheard-of passion. And now he himself had shown feelings deeper and more moving than anyone she had known before.

"I suppose," replied Sir Justin slowly, "that it was my father."

"Was he also . . ." She paused in confusion.

"A radical?" He chuckled. "In his way I suppose he was, though not as I am. He was much more respectable." Keighley's smile lingered. "He was inspired by the French Revolution in the beginning. That will shock you. He was an idealist who thought he saw his theories coming to life, only to be forced to watch their failure. That would have discouraged many men, I imagine, but not he. He carried on."

"What did he do?"

"Oh, all manner of things. He wrote pamphlets and books. He spoke wherever they would have him. He even went abroad to see conditions for himself, and very nearly did not get back, I understand." He grimaced. "I have never seen my mother so angry as when she speaks of that incident."

"Was he in Parliament?"

"No, indeed. He was not the sort of man to attract votes. Most of his neighbors thought him a bit mad." Keighley's tone was warm.

Margaret wondered at it. He sounded like a very odd sort of father. "He was busy with your estate, I suppose. It is large."

"Passably. But he never concerned himself with it for more than five minutes at a time, as far as I know. My mother managed everything, superbly. She is amazingly sharp. I have always thought that my grandfather must have chosen her for his son because of her wits, though she was not bad-looking." He chuckled again.

"They were a pair, my parents. I'm certain they were very attached to each other. I remember them so. My mother took care of all the practical details of living while my father spent his days dreaming in his study, and sometimes writing. When they met at dinner, each was remarkably happy, having passed the time as he wished. And the conversations at that table! I always joined them when there were no guests, from the very first, and I can remember endless, passionate debates about everything under the sun. They were both people of strong opinions, and they loved airing and defending them. Sometimes I think they took opposite sides just for the joy of battle. My sister and I plunged headlong into it as soon as we were able."

Fascinated, Margaret compared this vivid vision to the dinner-table conversations of her childhood. The contrast was marked.

"Do your parents never debate politics?" asked Keighley curiously. "Among their friends, I mean. I would not expect them to do so with me."

"They do," responded Margaret doubtfully. "But not in the way you describe."

"Ah?"

"They all seem to agree from the start. I mean, they do discuss things, but they only say how right their position is and how wrong that of the others. There isn't any . . . battle."

"I see." Keighley's tone was dry. "Well, I think that answers your question. I was taught that no idea is right until it is proved against the strongest and cleverest opposition. That is why I 'talk as I do.' I am championing my position against all comers. I cannot help throwing every resource at my command into the effort."

Margaret nodded slowly, taking this in. He watched her, wondering for the first time what it must have been like to grow up in the Mayfield household. For him it would have been hell. Or would it? He would not have known anything else, as Margaret had not. He tried to imagine such a life, and could not.

"What did you talk to your parents about?" he asked her.

She looked up, startled. "I?"

"Yes. You must have had other topics besides politics."

"Well . . . they always asked about my studies, when I was younger. I had a governess, and they would review my progress at the end of each week. A special time was set aside for it. And, of course, my mother taught me a great deal about running a household and . . . and that sort of thing."

"And you had friends in the neighborhood, I suppose." Keighley strained to recollect. "The Camden girl, and so on."

Margaret shrugged. "I was very busy with my studies. Mama felt that they were more important, though my governess and I took ample outdoor exercise."

For the first time Sir Justin felt something other than impatience or anger with the girl. Clearly she had some excuse for her shortcomings. He pitied her sincerely for her bland, sterile upbringing. He himself would no doubt have gone mad in such an environment or driven his tormentors mad. This vision brought a brief smile to his face, but it faded when he met Margaret's anxious gaze. If it were not for his own damnable involvement, he could almost have been glad for the incidents that had made this girl flee her home. It could only help her to be away from it. Indeed, it *had* helped, as he had already observed.

"I was not unhappy," said Margaret to prevent a false impression.

No, thought Keighley, you were never allowed even that much.

Margaret frowned at him, not understanding his expression in the least. In anyone else she might have labeled it sadness, but that was clearly impossible in this case.

"Are you tired?" she ventured. "You shouldn't sit up too long."

He looked up again and felt a sudden twinge of warning. Their situation *was* damnable, and he would do nothing to improve it by starting to pity the girl or worry over her. He knew only too well where that sort of thing could lead, and he wanted no part of it. "I am, rather," he answered. "Perhaps you should fetch Appleby to help me upstairs."

9

The three days following this evening passed quietly. Keighley withdrew into himself and encouraged Margaret to leave him alone and walk. He talked no more of boredom, and she would often find Jemmy Appleby with him when she came in from striding along the beach. Sir Justin seemed fond of the boy, and Jemmy was obviously overcome by his favor. Margaret told herself that she should be glad her patient needed her less, but in fact she felt rather slighted and shut out. The kindlier impulses toward Keighley that had surfaced during their conversations were thwarted. She could not understand why he was so pleasant one day and so indifferent the next.

She channeled her puzzlement into her walks, going farther than before and moving faster. The increased exercise hastened the process begun earlier, and Margaret's face gained animation and life as her form strengthened and rounded. Her appetite now required no tempting, and she began to find her formerly loose gowns a better fit. She could not help noticing the change, and had she been so blind, Mrs. Appleby's encouraging comments would have made it clear to her that her appearance was greatly improved.

On the fourth morning Keighley called her to his room first thing, and she went eagerly, wondering if his distant mood had changed. But he said only, "I am sending young Appleby to Falmouth for some clothes and other necessities. Tell him what you need, or have his mother do so, and he can get that as well. The workmanship will be inferior, I suppose, but it will be better than nothing."

"I . . . I have all I need."

"Indeed? You surprise me."

His tone annoyed Margaret, so she added, "Very well, I do not, then. But I haven't much money. I shall get along with what I brought."

"Ah. Fortunately I took the precaution of bringing a substantial sum with me."

"You cannot buy me clothes."

He shrugged. "Since I will in all probability be paying for this inn and for transportation away from it, I cannot see that it matters."

She flushed. "I mean to pay my share. I . . . I can manage that."

"And have nothing left?" He gazed at her, his curiosity roused in spite of himself. "What did you intend, running away with so little money?"

"It was all I could get together without asking," replied Margaret defensively. "I planned to find a position at once and support myself." He looked so skeptical that she added, "I could be a governess, you know. I know Italian and music and drawing and—"

"Of course." His dismissive tone made her bite her lower lip. Of course he did not care what she did. "If you will just speak to Jemmy, then?" he finished. "I believe he wished to start as soon as possible."

Margaret nodded and turned away from him, wholly unaware that he had cut her off because he had once again begun to pity her. She found Jemmy, made her requests, and retreated to her favorite spot on the beach.

She did not see Keighley again that day. He sent word that he was tired and would eat his dinner alone, which suited her down to the ground, Margaret told herself fiercely. She ate in the parlor and went to bed early, ignoring the sounds of Jemmy's return somewhat later. Let Keighley be alone; he could be alone forever, as far as she was concerned.

But the following morning, when she found him standing with Jemmy on the threshold of the inn dressed to go out, she could not help but protest.

"What are you doing?"

"Preparing to take a short stroll," was the reply.

"Do you feel well enough? Are you sure you should?"

"Obviously, since I am here, I do. I must get some exercise if I am ever to recover, and I think we would both agree that the sooner I do, the better."

"Of course," answered Margaret stiffly. "I will come with you."

"There is no need. Jem is accompanying me."

"I see that he is. I shall come, too."

"It really is *not* necessary."

"Perhaps it isn't, but I am not going to sit here and worry about whether you have fallen into the sea."

"You prefer to have the pleasure of witnessing the event."

She glared at him. "Yes! I hope I may."

"Indeed, your sister *should* go with you, Mr. Camden," said a voice above them. They all looked up to find Mrs. Appleby leaning out a first-floor window. "Jem's a good lad, but heedless. I'll feel easier if she goes."

Keighley bowed his head and turned away. "Did you find me that stick, Jem?" was his only comment.

"Yessir. Here it is." The boy handed him a thick walking stick.

"Good. Well, it appears we are ready, then."

"I'll just get my hat," said Margaret.

"We will start out. You can catch up when you are ready."

She started to object, then shrugged impatiently and ran for her bonnet.

They were halfway down to the seawall before she joined them, and no one spoke until they stood looking out over the waves. Then Keighley said, "A fair day."

"It is that, sir," replied Jemmy eagerly. "Just the sort of day to take out the *Gull*."

Margaret started to protest. Sir Justin was by no means well enough to sail. But he forestalled her. "I wish I might. But this cursed arm won't stand it yet."

Jemmy's face fell. "No, sir."

"We could have a look at her, however. Where is she berthed?"

"In Rook's Inlet," answered the boy quickly. "I usually keep her down at the docks, but I left her there because it was closer and I was in a hurry. It ain't far."

Keighley laughed. "Let us go, then, by all means."

Jem gave a whoop and leaped to the top of the seawall. "This way," he cried, racing along it.

"Be careful," Margaret called.

Jemmy didn't hear, but Keighley said, "He has no doubt been doing that since he could climb it." She subsided.

They walked along the curve of the wall, Jem running ahead and coming back like an eager spaniel. Keighley did not speak, but he took deep breaths of the sparkling sea air. It was a perfect day. The sun shone glittering on the waves, and the flowering plants in the village shed their fragrance everywhere. A mild ocean breeze kept it from being hot and stirred the leaves, one's hair and clothing, and the line of foam on the sand below. Margaret found herself emulating her companion and drawing in deep lungfuls of air. Something made her want to skip or fling out her arms and whirl round and round.

When they reached the steps in the seawall and started down, Margaret suddenly realized the probable identity of Rook's Inlet and made an involuntary sound. "What is it?" said Keighley, turning to look at her.

"Nothing. That is, I believe I know where we are going. I . . . I discovered it on one of my first walks here."

"Really?" He turned away again and started slowly along the sand. He appeared to find the footing difficult.

"Are you all right?" asked Margaret, hurrying to catch up.

"Yes, yes. Come along. Jem has left us far behind."

She followed him anxiously, watching as he dug the walking stick deep into the sand at each step. She thought he looked paler and wondered how she would get him back to the inn if he fainted.

But they made it to the inlet well enough. As she had suspected, it was the spot she had earlier discovered. Today there was a small boat moored in the opening, dispelling the flavor of secrecy, as did Jemmy's eager babble of information.

Margaret eyed the craft with approval. From some of the boy's remarks she had expected a ramshackle boat, but the *Gull* was painted cheerful yellow and innocent of any speck of dirt. It was small—only about fifteen feet, she guessed—but the front third had been decked over to form a tiny cabin or storage nook, and there were things like cupboards along the sides behind it. The sail was neatly furled about the mast, and the craft generally looked as if care had been lavished upon it. "How pretty," she said.

Jemmy looked torn between pride at the compliment and contempt for the unprofessional judgment.

"A fine little vessel," agreed Keighley, who had been leaning over it while the boy showed him all the amenities. "Did you fit her out yourself?"

"Yes, sir. That is, my brother helped me with the carpentry. I did all the rest."

"Good for you. How does she head?"

"Pretty well, considering," responded Jem quickly. "She's a bit broad."

As they again became immersed in technicalities Margaret wandered back into the depths of the inlet. The pool was as serenely quiet as ever; the flowering vine hung over it, and the trickle of water wet the cliff. She sank down with a sigh and let the silence wash over her.

Some minutes passed; she did not notice exactly how long. She was content merely to sit. Then, though she had heard no approach, a deep voice said, "A peaceful spot."

Margaret started and looked up to find Keighley standing only a few feet away. "Yes. I come here often. I found it on my first walk."

He took a step closer and looked about. "I can see why you like it. Do I disturb you?"

"No." She was a little surprised that he would ask.

"It's amazingly cool."

"It always is. I think it must be the water."

He watched the trickle down the cliff face and nodded. The silence descended again.

At first Margaret felt as if she should speak, though she could think of nothing to say. It seemed awkward to sit quietly with Keighley so close. But after a moment this feeling left her. The peace of the place seemed to flood back, and she relaxed once more in the seat she had made of two flat stones. She dared to look up and discovered a new expression on Sir Justin's face. His dark brows and rugged features were smoothed in a calm she had never before glimpsed about him; he looked approachable and—she struggled to define what she saw— happy in a quiet, inner way. His face seemed to mirror what Margaret had often felt in this place, and for a brief instant she felt close to him. She knew what was passing through his heart.

"Sir," called an urgent voice. "Mr. Camden, sir. I've found it."

Keighley started slightly, looked down at her, and smiled. "Jem has further wonders to show. Thank you."

"For what?"

"For sharing your discovery." With this, he turned away and disappeared through the fringe of leaves. Margaret sat still a moment longer, then jumped to her feet and followed.

Jem Appleby was going through the various compartments of his boat, showing Sir Justin all his equipment. When Margaret joined them, he included her peripherally, as if wishing to be polite while acknowledging that she was not deeply interested. When at last they had seen everything and the display was again neatly stowed, Jem stepped reluctantly back to shore. "I do wish we could take her out," he said again. "We don't get a breeze like this every day."

Keighley nodded sympathetically.

"You could go out," suggested Margaret. "I can see, er, Harry back to the inn."

The boy looked tempted, then shook his head. "Ma has chores for me. She said so when I left. Perhaps later."

He looked so disappointed that Margaret could not help adding, "I'm sorry."

Sir Justin was smiling. "By the by, Margaret, I don't believe you have ever been on a boat."

Startled, she began to shake her head, when Jemmy exclaimed, "Ain't you taken her on yours, sir?"

"Er, yes. I meant to say, on such a small boat. Don't you want to go aboard and see how it feels?"

"You're welcome, miss," said Jemmy. "She's quiet now. Not much roll."

He gazed at her with eager blue eyes as Margaret frowned at the gently rocking *Gull*. It looked frighteningly unsteady. Raising her eyes, she met Sir Justin's. He was mocking her. "I'd like to," replied Margaret stoutly. "But I am not sure how . . ."

"I'll help you." The boy came forward. "I wish she were at the dock, but I'll pull her in so you won't get your shoes wet." He proceeded to draw the prow of the boat up onto the sand. "Just sit there," he indicated. Margaret obediently sat on the roof of the tiny cabin, which was flush with the sides of the craft. "Now, pull your legs up, and I'll push you off so's you can get a feel for her."

She lifted her legs into the well behind her seat. Jem shoved, and the *Gull* slowly slid down the sand and into the blue water. In a moment it was floating free. Involuntarily Margaret gasped.

"Don't worry," called Jemmy. "She's tied. Don't she ride nice, though?"

Margaret took several deep breaths. She started to shift her position, but when the boat rocked in response, she desisted. It was disconcerting to be on a platform that continually tilted. She looked to shore. Jemmy was watching her with expectant pride, and Keighley was clearly stifling laughter. Margaret straightened. "It's . . . very nice," she told the boy, who nodded with pleasure. And even as she spoke she realized that it was true. The boat rose and fell soothingly beneath her; the sun shone warm and the breeze cooled her face. The constant motion made her feel very free. "It's lovely," she added with obvious enthusiasm, and Jemmy grinned while Keighley let his laugh out. It was a pleasant laugh, Margaret saw now, not mocking at all, and she joined him gaily.

She was sorry when Jem hauled her in again and helped her out of the *Gull*. "Thank you," she said to him. "It is a beautiful boat. I should like to go out in it sometime, if you will let me."

"Oh, yes, miss. I'll take you both."

Margaret smiled up at Keighley, but a shadow had passed over his face, and he turned away. "We'd best get back," he said.

They trudged across the sand in silence. Jem bounded up the stairs in the seawall and ran along the top while Margaret followed more slowly. At the head of the steps she paused and looked back. Sir Justin was leaning heavily against the wall about halfway up. His face was ashen, and his breath came in gasps. She hurried to his side. "Are you all right? What is it?"

"Nothing. I've just . . . overdone it a trifle . . . it seems."

"I'll help you." She put a hand under his elbow.

"A moment." He breathed sonorously several times. "All right."

Very slowly they made their way up, stopping twice for Keighley to rest. At the top Margaret looked about anxiously. "Oh, where has Jemmy gone? I must send him for his father."

"No need," replied Keighley raspingly.

"Nonsense. I will go. You sit here and wait for us."

"No!"

His tone was so sharp that she stopped in midstride.

"I can get back on my own. I won't be fetched like some invalid. It was just the stairs."

Margaret eyed him. His breathing was easier now, but he was still alarmingly white. "You have a serious wound," she began.

"I can walk back to the inn," he interrupted. "I *must* recover my strength, and I shall never do so lying on my back."

"Nor by overtaxing yourself before you are ready," she retorted tartly.

"I am ready." He straightened and moved away from

the wall. "Go on ahead if you like. I shall be along directly."

With an angry sigh, she came to take his elbow again. "Of course I am likely to leave you here, aren't I? How stubborn you are. Come along."

With a wry smile, he allowed her to guide him down the cobbled road to the lane that led up to the inn. "Won't you wait here?" pleaded Margaret then. "This climb is longer than the stairs. I'll get Mr. Appleby."

Grimly he shook his head.

Margaret sighed again. If he would not promise to stay still, she could not leave him. She tightened her grip on his elbow. "Very well."

They had not covered half the distance when Keighley suddenly swayed against her, dropping his walking stick with a clatter. Margaret threw an arm about his waist to support the added weight and cried, "What is it?"

"Shoulder," he murmured, putting a hand to his wound.

Desperately she looked about for help. But they were in a section of road without doorways, and there were no pedestrians in sight. Mustering all her strength, she inserted her shoulder in Sir Justin's unhurt armpit and said, "Put your arm about my shoulders. It is not much farther."

He did so, and they went on slowly in this way. He was breathing heavily again, and Margaret was terribly afraid she would fail him and let him fall. He was so heavy. She took another step, and another, more and more conscious of his ribs against her heaving breast, his muscular arm across her shoulders. She tried to look up at his face, to gauge his condition, but a fold of his coat obscured her eyes and she got only a breath of his scent, compounded of leather, tobacco, and something unfamiliar.

They came around a corner, and Margaret saw Jemmy a little ahead, skipping back in their direction. "Jemmy," she shouted, "get your father. Quickly!"

After one round-eyed glance, the boy turned and pelted off toward the inn. "There," said Margaret. "Soon we will have help."

"Wanted to make it on my own," muttered Keighley.

"It was too soon, that is all. Come, will you sit on that bench?"

"No. Stand."

Though she found his insistence incomprehensible, Margaret could not argue with him. But she did stop walking. Pressed together, they swayed in the middle of the street waiting for aid to arrive. Keighley seemed hardly aware of their surroundings, but Margaret found her perceptions unusually sharp in the slow minutes she supported his sagging frame.

She had wondered before at the unaccustomed emotions Keighley roused in her, emotions of a strength she had never experienced. That most of them had been negative feelings—anger, exasperation, pique—did not lessen her perplexity. But now she felt something new. Beneath her sharp concern for her patient's condition, some unidentifiable stirring lurked. It was not an emotion, or at least none she recognized, but some hitherto-untouched part of her seemed to be awakening. The sensation confused her and kept her silent as they stood together on the hot stones.

She felt keenly that she needed time to herself to think. The changes in her appearance and situation were being echoed by alterations in her opinions and outlook, but she had not yet examined and understood the latter, and this made her uneasy. She knew that she *had* hated and feared Sir Justin Keighley. But she was fairly certain that those feelings were now gone forever. What had replaced them? This was by no means as clear. He could still make her blazingly angry, and she still found his political position unconvincing. But the man himself—

she didn't know what she thought of him. Standing there with her arm about his waist and his side pressed against hers, she found this question both unanswerable and vitally important.

10

Sir Justin had to spend the rest of that day and all of the following one in bed, unable to come downstairs for dinner. Margaret, worried, called in Mrs. Dowling, who shook her head and scolded her patient soundly but told the girl that she needn't be really concerned. "He's just worn himself out, dearie, as men will do. He'll be all right once he rests."

Thus reassured, Margaret slept soundly through the night, but when she she entered Keighley's room the next morning, his pallor alarmed her anew, and his manner when she bid him good day added to her concern. He seemed uncharacteristically listless.

"How are you feeling?" she asked.

He half shrugged, moving only his uninjured shoulder.

"Can I get you anything?"

He shook his head apathetically.

"Are you sure? You look so . . . so tired. Perhaps I should send for Mrs. Dowling to have another look at you."

"There is no need for that."

Margaret frowned at him. She had never heard him speak with so little force or interest. He seemed not to care what happened, which was not at all like him.

"Shall I get the cards?" she ventured, thinking to arouse irritation, at least. "I have counted them, and the jack of hearts *is* missing, but I made a substitute."

"I don't think I'm up to cards today."

"Not up to playing with *me*, you mean. But I have been practicing." She tried a smile, but he did not respond. "Oh, what is the matter? You are feeling worse, aren't you? I shall go for Mrs. Dowling at once." She half rose.

"I am feeling just as I did yesterday afternoon," he replied savagely, "hardly able to lift my head from the pillow. It is intolerable!"

Margaret sank back into the armchair. "But Mrs. Dowling said it was nothing but overexertion. It will pass off in a day or so. You merely tried to do too much too soon."

"Too much," he echoed bitterly. "Do you know that this has never happened to me in my life before? I have never found my strength inadequate to anything I wished to undertake, and it galls me beyond bearing."

"But . . . you were wounded. You cannot expect to be well in a moment. It is only natural that you should be weak."

"It is not natural to *me*." He paused and almost seemed to grind his teeth. "Yesterday, coming up that hill, I actually *could not* make it. It was not a matter of will—my body failed me. It has *never* done so before."

Margaret found the intensity of his tone strange. Of course it must be annoying to feel so weak, but it was only temporary. "Well, I daresay you have never been shot before," she replied. "Mrs. Dowling says that you will be able to get up again tomorrow, for a short time, and then—"

"That is completely beside the point," he snapped. "Oh, why do I waste my time talking to you? You understand nothing." He turned his head away from her.

Margaret frowned at him again. "Perhaps not. But I would like to. Won't you tell me what you mean?"

There was a silence as he considered her request. He was tired, too tired to resist the comfort of sharing his frustrations with another human being, even when he knew he should not encourage any closeness between them. He sighed. "I am accustomed to being in control of my life," he began. "I go where I please. I do and say what I please. I follow only my own inclinations. Now, suddenly, all that is at an end. I am confined to this wretched bed, this inn, this village. There is little to amuse me, and what there is I cannot do because of physical weakness. I can hardly *feed* myself today. Everything must be done for me. I must ask others for the smallest necessity. Can you not see how hard that is to endure?"

"I suppose so," said Margaret slowly. "But we are glad to help you, you know."

"Yes, indeed. It might be easier if you begrudged your service."

She gazed at him in perplexity.

"Have you never felt chafed by others' direction?" he added. "I have all my life. I have never allowed anyone to control me."

Margaret smiled. "Never? What about your parents? Surely when you were small they guided you."

Keighley's expression relaxed a little. He shook his head. "My father, never. He did not even try. I think he lacked not only the wish but even the conception. He cared nothing for power over others. His sole passion was knowledge and ideas. My mother was another matter." He smiled. "She used to box my ears now and then, and once I remember a thrashing. But I didn't pay the least heed. I did what I wished and took the consequences gladly."

"What a dreadful little boy you must have been."

He laughed. "I know my sister thought so. But I suspect that was only because she was so like me. We never played together without quarreling over who should be chief and make the rules of the game."

"Did you never wonder if your mother might know best?"

"No." He laughed again.

Margaret pondered this alien vision of childhood. "How strange. *I* never considered that she mightn't. I always did as I was told, without question. Why, do you suppose? I *ought* to have wondered."

He shrugged. "A matter of temperament."

"You mean I was born so? And you were born a . . . a radical?"

This time his laugh was hearty. "I suppose I was."

She looked down at her hands in her lap. "It seems unfair. Why should one person be so docile and another so rebellious? I would have objected . . . if I had *thought* of it."

Keighley surveyed her with a mixture of amusement and interest. "You did, finally."

She met his hazel eyes. "I did—that's right."

He raised one black brow.

Margaret thought this over. "And if I could suddenly alter my behavior, surely you can tolerate a few days of a different sort of life. You might even enjoy them, if you let yourself." She cocked her head and watched him inquiringly.

Sir Justin stared at her. The girl actually had a good point. He found her suggestion annoying, but he had to admit that there was something in it. Could this really be the same brainless chit he had set out to drag home? Could anyone change *that* much in such a short time?

Margaret burst out laughing. "You look stupefied," she sputtered. "I never thought to see you silenced so thoroughly."

"Did you not?"

She shook her head, still laughing.

"The sight does not appear to sadden you, however."

"Oh, no. I think it must be very good for you—just like lying in bed for a day or so."

"I see. And what other horrors are in store for me at your hands?"

"None," responded Margaret cheerfully. "I have found that one must take these changes slowly. And do you know what I have just remembered?"

"I hesitate to ask."

"Your books. Didn't Jemmy bring back some books with the clothes from Falmouth?"

"By Jove, so he did. I had forgotten. How right I was to order them. And how fortunate that Falmouth boasts a bookseller. Let us have them brought up at once. There is something for you in the package as well."

Margaret jumped up. "In that case, I'll get them myself."

She hurried out. Sir Justin gazed at the empty doorway and wondered if he was being dangerously foolish. If anyone had told him a month ago that he would trade intimate banter with a chit barely out of the schoolroom, he would have advised them kindly to give up strong spirits and take a rest cure. And yet it had seemed very natural as it was happening. It must be this damnable weakness that was making him behave so. He had to recover, as quickly as possible.

"Here they are," called Margaret, returning with a large bundle wrapped in brown paper. She plumped it down on the table beside his bed and began to struggle with the knot.

"You need a knife," said Keighley. "I think mine is on the washstand."

She nodded and fetched it, cutting through the string in three places. The paper fell away to reveal two stacks of books. With a sigh of satisfaction, she knelt to examine them.

Keighley laboriously pushed himself straighter on the pillows. "There should be some novels and a history, and something else I ordered particularly for you."

"What?" She had finished reading the titles in the first stack and was moving it to get to the second.

"I think you will recognize it when you come upon it."

She kept scanning the volumes. "Oh. Not . . . is it this one?" She pulled out a fat, leatherbound book. "*An Examination of the Need for and Principles of Reform of the English Governmental System.*"

"That's the one." Their eyes met, and he laughed at her expression. "You needn't read it if you don't wish to, but after our discussion recently I thought you might."

Margaret looked longingly at the four novels on the table. She had never read any of them or, indeed, seen so many fictional works at one time in her parents' house. But as she remembered the conversation he referred to, her brows drew together. "I suppose it was written by someone who agrees with your opinions?" she asked.

"Of course. I would hardly push your own back on you."

"Well, I will read it, and I shall tell you what I think when I am done," she said, almost belligerently.

"Splendid."

"I daresay I won't like it at all."

"Probably not. But one never knows. You have been advocating change in an astonishingly radical way."

Margaret opened her mouth to protest, then smiled instead. "That is not precisely the same thing."

"Is it not?"

"No." She was sure it wasn't, but not certain why.

He gestured dismissively. "Let's see what you say when you have finished the book."

She clutched the volume to her chest, gazing down at it uneasily. It was very long.

"You'll want to start at once, I suppose. And I have been wanting to read this novel for weeks." With an effort, he reached out and took a book from the top of one stack. "We will spend a quiet, profitable morning in study."

Margaret eyed him suspiciously, but he returned her glance with no hint of mockery. At last she nodded and turned toward the door.

"We can discuss the first part over luncheon," he added. "I shall look forward to it."

Margaret merely tossed her head and left the room, making Keighley smile and suppress a laugh.

She read dutifully for an hour in the parlor downstairs, but the book was heavy going. The author would make an interesting point and then, so it seemed to Margaret, go on for pages about mostly irrelevant incidents in order to prove it. She began skipping over paragraphs, and finally whole pages, and at last she put the book down and rose to stretch wearily.

She went to the parlor window. It was another sunny day; they had had a long period of fine weather. With a guilty glance at the book on the sofa, Margaret decided she would go out for a walk—a short one.

She went down to the seawall and along the route they had taken yesterday. Jemmy's boat was no longer in the inlet. She sat for a while beside her pool, then turned back. She should read a little more before luncheon, though Keighley had surely been joking when he said they would discuss it.

When she reached the lane that led back up toward the inn, Margaret remembered something that caused her to take another turning. She had not been back to speak to Mrs. Dowling, and she still wanted to see her, for several reasons. She found the old woman's cottage without trouble and knocked on the door. It was opened by an attractive, smiling woman of about forty with red-brown hair and sparkling brown eyes. Margaret blinked in surprise and momentary disorientation. Had she come to the wrong house? But this woman resembled Mrs. Dowling; in fact, for a moment it seemed that she was seeing Mrs. Dowling as she had been—or perhaps as she really was.

This illusion was dispelled when the woman said, "Hello. You must be the young lady at the Red Lion. Mother was telling me about you. Come in. I hope there's no trouble?"

"N-no. I was just, er, coming to see Mrs. Dowling."

"Isn't that kind. She'll be happy to have you, I'm sure. She stepped out for a moment, but she'll be back directly. Come in and sit down." Seeing Margaret's dazed look, she added, "I'm her daughter, you know. I'm here for a visit from Falmouth, where I live."

"Oh, yes. How do you do?"

"I'm afraid I've promised to see some friends just now, but as I said, Mother will be back in a moment. If you wouldn't mind waiting alone?"

"No, not at all." Margaret was too flustered to do anything but agree.

"Good. It'll only be a bit." And with a pleasant nod, the woman picked up her bonnet and departed.

When she was gone, Margaret stared bemusedly at the wall. What a strange feeling that had been—when she thought she was facing a younger Mrs. Dowling. Why had she reacted that way? It was logical that Mrs. Dowling would have children and that they should visit her—yes, resemble her, too. Why should she jump to such conclusions? Margaret realized then that her first Mrs. Dowling had radically altered her view of the Instead of thinking of her as an old witch, a she was now heartily ashamed of, she now saw a wiser, older woman, rather like her daughter had appeared. How strange that such a change should come after one talk.

Footsteps sounded outside, the latch rattled, and Mrs. Dowling herself came in. When she saw Margaret, she smiled. "Well, now, miss. And I expected to find the place empty when I came back. This *is* pleasant."

Margaret had stood at her entrance. "I just stopped in on my way . . . Your daughter said I might wait."

"Did you meet Carrie, then?" replied the old woman, removing her black bonnet. "She's a fine girl—my eldest. Can I get you some tea?"

"Oh, no, thank you."

Mrs. Dowling eyed her. "Let's go out back. The sun's not too hot yet."

Margaret followed her onto the terrace, and they sat on the low wall looking out over the sea.

"You're bothered about summat, bain't you, dearie? The gentleman's not worse?"

"No. He's weak but all right."

Mrs. Dowling nodded. "As I told you. These men *will* get up before they're able."

Seizing this opening, Margaret blurted, "You seem to know a great deal about men." As soon as the words were out, she regretted them. She blushed fiercely and looked down at the flagstones between her feet.

Mrs. Dowling chuckled. "I should. I've nursed a deal of them, and I was married thirty years. Feeling puzzled, are you, miss?"

Margaret twisted her hands in her lap and wished she hadn't come.

"Nothing strange in that. Women have been puzzling over men since the beginning, I expect. And men over women—perhaps more. What can I tell ye?"

Realizing that she hadn't the slightest idea, Margaret turned to gaze out over the blue ocean. She had questions, but they were so bewildering that she was not even certain how to put them. She wished again that she hadn't come. What had made her suppose that Mrs. Dowling, kind as she might be, could help her?

"Is it something about your, ah, brother?" inquired the old woman.

Her tone reminded Margaret of something. "You mustn't go about telling people that he is not my brother," she said. "Of course he is."

"I don't gossip about the village," replied Mrs. Dowling quietly, with a dignity that made her listener shrink down a bit. "In my position I hear a good many things folks wouldn't want talked of. And nary a word passes my lips unless to someone who can help. I've spoken to the reverend over to Falmouth once, and to a husband or two, but no other. My mother was midwife before me, and she always said, 'A loose tongue is worse than an unsteady hand in this business, Carrie.' I've held to that."

"I . . . I'm sorry. I didn't mean . . ."

"You weren't to know. There's some as chatter everything they see. But not I." She lowered her gaze, which had been fixed sternly on a pot of pink geraniums. "If there was something you wanted to ask me, miss, it wouldn't go no further."

But Margaret was by now too embarrassed to ask anything. "No, there's nothing. But . . . thank you. I should go now."

Mrs. Dowling rose to stand beside her, her white head reaching only just above the girl's shoulder. "You know best. I'm usually about the cottage in the afternoons. Mornings, I see to my patients."

She led Margaret to the front door and saw her out.

"Th-Thank you," stammered Margaret again, though she was unsure why.

The old woman grinned, bobbed her head, and shut the door.

Walking back up to the Red Lion, Margaret wondered

at herself. What had she expected to accomplish by *that* ill-conceived visit? And what was wrong with her? She had been rather complacently pleased with the changes in herself recently—with her newfound confidence and her altered looks. But with Mrs. Dowling today, she had felt sillier than she ever had at home. How could she imagine that an old village midwife could advise her about problems she could not even define? Assuming that the woman had useful knowledge, a thing Margaret was not at all sure of at this moment, she could not be expected to read thoughts from the air as well. It was becoming imperative that Margaret understand and order her feelings, and she did not know where to begin.

11

Three weeks to the day after Sir Justin Keighley had been carried to the Red Lion, a curious expedition left it early one August morning. It consisted first of Jemmy Appleby, liberally laden with baskets, parcels, and rugs, then of Margaret, also carrying several bundles, and finally of Sir Justin, who held nothing but a walking stick. The day was fine, and they were at last gratifying Jem's urgent wish to take them out in the *Gull*.

The decision to make the excursion had not been easy. Keighley, who had scrupulously followed Mrs. Dowling's orders and hardly ventured from his room for days, had at last insisted that he was well enough to go out again, and that he would go quite mad if he were shut up any longer. Margaret, while expressing sympathy with his desire, had argued against sailing with all her eloquence. She could not think it wise for Keighley to so cut himself off from help. However, when she found that he meant to go without her, she sighed and gave in. Mrs. Dowling had after all said that Sir Justin was greatly improved.

And so a series of quiet days came to an end with this outing. Margaret had been spending her time reading— she had finished the book Keighley had given her—and thinking. Neither had been wholly satisfactory. The book left her mind whirling with new ideas, some of which she approved and others she resisted, and her efforts to understand her own mental condition generally ended in confusion as well. After a time she had abandoned the latter attempt. Things were peaceful; there seemed no need to agonize.

Jem had brought his boat into the inlet again, as it was closer than the docks on the other side of the village. He led them there, chattering eagerly the whole time, and deposited his various burdens on the shore. "You can put the other things there as well, miss," he said. "I'll begin stowing them in a minute."

Gratefully Margaret put down her bundles. The boy started to check over his craft, with Keighley watching smilingly, and she strolled out to the head of the inlet to look at the bay. The water was calm under a broad blue sky. A soft breeze blew in her face. This was good, she knew, having received some cursory instructions from Keighley the previous evening. Without any wind the boat would not move, but with too much such a small craft could be dangerous.

"Come on, miss," called Jemmy, and she returned to find that all the packages had somehow been fitted into the *Gull*'s compartments. "You can get aboard now," added the boy. Keighley was bent over the mooring rope, farther up the beach.

Gathering up the skirts of her light blue cambric gown, Margaret climbed into the boat as she had been instructed on the previous occasion. Jemmy put a steadying hand under her elbow and, when she was sitting on the decking over the tiny cabin, said, "Move on back, miss, and sit on top of one of those lockers."

Margaret looked around, puzzled.

"The compartments on the side, miss."

"Oh." Carefully she edged her way along the deck, lowered her feet into the boat, and swiveled around to sit on one of the cupboards. The *Gull* rocked abruptly as she did so, and Margaret clutched the side behind her.

"That's it," said Jemmy encouragingly. "We're ready for you, sir."

Keighley joined him, handing over the mooring line. "Shall I help you shove her off?"

"I'll do it, sir."

"I doubt you can with both of us aboard. Let us push her out a bit first."

Jemmy shrugged his agreement, and the two of them pushed the boat farther out into the water. Margaret felt the back float free, a curious sensation. Keighley leaped lightly in on the side opposite her and looked ruefully down at his wet riding boots. "My valet will have something to say about that. Salt water. I wish I had some other footgear."

"I thought you were going to borrow Jem's brother's boots."

"Unfortunately his feet turned out to be a good deal smaller than mine."

Jemmy was straining at the boat, shoving it away from the shore until he stood in water up to his knees. "I'm going to pull her out with the line, sir," he said then. "Will you take the tiller?"

Nodding, Keighley moved to the rear of the craft and put his hand on a rod there. "Does that steer the boat?" asked Margaret.

"Yes. It is attached to the rudder."

Jem heaved again, and the *Gull* slid toward the mouth of the inlet. Margaret was pleasantly surprised by the smooth glide; it was quite unlike the ride of any other vehicle she knew. When they had passed out into the bay and the water started to deepen, Jem hauled himself in and wrung out the bottoms of his trousers. "Sorry, miss," he muttered when a rivulet of water threatened to wet her skirts.

"That's all right," replied Margaret stoutly. "I expect I shall get wet before the day is out."

Keighley grinned at her, and Jem bobbed his head before clambering up to free the sail. It was small and soon raised, a triangle of white above their heads. "All right, sir," said the boy when it was secure. "We head nor'east." He pointed, and Sir Justin eased the tiller over. Margaret watched, enthralled, as the wind belled out the sail and their speed increased. But then the *Gull* began to lean sideways, tilting the side where she sat toward the waves, and she could not restrain a muffled cry. The water seemed so close.

"It's all right," Keighley assured her. "The wind in the sail makes it lean. But you'll probably want to sit on the other side now."

Gingerly Margaret shifted seats. It did indeed feel much safer on the opposite side.

"Will you take the helm, Captain?" said Sir Justin to Jemmy, and with a wide smile the boy moved to do so. Keighley slid up to the front decking. "She runs well," he added, gazing about.

Jem beamed with pride.

"Where are we going?" Margaret asked him.

"There's a little island in the bay. No one lives there— too small and there's no water. But it's a good spot for picnics, Ma says, and it's a fine sail."

Nodding, she turned back to the view. The wind was stronger out here on the water, and the little boat seemed to be flying along. The sun sparkled on the waves and danced over the trail of foam they left behind. A real gull flew over, crying sadly. Margaret felt exhilarated. "This is wonderful," she said.

Sir Justin turned to smile at her. "It is not always quite so pleasant, is it, Jem?"

"Nossir." The boy grinned.

"Before you can claim to like it, you must go out in

rain and high seas, *and* in a wind so stiff that the boat nearly comes out of water."

"Why?"

"The force of the air on the sail pushes—"

"No, no, I mean why must I do those things? They sound dreadful."

He laughed. "To be a true sailor, you must be able to face the sea in all its moods."

"A fair-weather sailor don't know anything," agreed Jemmy.

"Perhaps not," responded Margaret, "but I daresay he is much happier."

Keighley laughed again. "A friend of mine who has a beautiful yacht insists that anyone who wishes to know what owning a boat is like need only stand outside in a cold rain and tear up pound notes. The effect is the same."

Margaret gazed at him with half-laughing incredulity.

"You are out in all weathers," he explained, "and you spend a great deal of money. What do you say, Jem?"

"I wish I had a few pound notes to spend on the *Gull*," replied the practical boy.

Margaret laughed. "Indeed. I think your friend is very silly. If that is the way he feels about it, he should do something else with his time."

Shaking his head, Sir Justin turned back to the sea.

"There's the island," said Jemmy, pointing.

Following his finger, Margaret could just see a smudge of land between them and the farther shore of the bay. "That was very fast."

"We aren't there yet," answered Keighley.

"But we are"—she looked back—"nearly halfway already."

"In distance, perhaps, but our journey will take quite a time yet."

Margaret soon found out what he meant. Instead of

sailing directly to the island, they went first to the left of it and then to the right. This maneuver, she was told, was called tacking, the sailor's mode of travel. A sailing vessel must follow the wind, and not its master's inclination.

Thus, a trip she had thought would take no more than half an hour stretched to two hours, and by the time they nosed in to land she had had enough of the sea for a while. She was also very hungry.

"There's a good place up above," said Jemmy when all their bundles had been unloaded and piled on the grass.

Margaret followed his gaze with a grimace. The island was one large hillock thrusting out of the water, and the climb to the top appeared steep. She was not overeager to attempt it hung with luggage, particularly before lunch. "It may be too taxing for you," she said to Keighley.

"Nonsense, I am not in the least fatigued. And the view should be splendid. Let us go up by all means."

With a sigh, she bent to pick up some rugs and a basket. Jem had already begun to festoon himself.

"I can take something," added Sir Justin with a smile.

"No, you go ahead. Mrs. Dowling said you weren't to carry things or go too fast."

With an amused shrug, he turned away and started up the hill. Jem followed, and Margaret brought up the rear, with the first of many silent curses at the flounced hem of her gown, which continually tried to trip her up.

Fortunately the ascent was not as arduous as it had appeared from water level. There was a good path winding back and forth across the hill, and the breeze kept the sun from feeling too hot. In ten minutes they had gained the summit, where a clump of four beech trees offered grassy shade. Margaret put down her bundles and straightened to look around, only to gasp with astonished pleasure. The panorama was breathtaking. The shore of the bay curved distantly around them on three sides, making a line of green between the blue water and the cloudless sky. Behind her the view was open to the sea, and here the blue stretched infinitely out and up. They could see the village, color-splashed white against the gray cliff, near the bay's mouth. Margaret let her breath out in a sigh. "I have never seen anything so lovely."

"It is," agreed Keighley. "Thank you for bringing us here, Jem."

"Oh, yes."

"Thought you'd like it," replied Jem complacently. "I'll set out the lunch, shall I?"

"Do," agreed Sir Justin, meeting Margaret's eyes with a laugh in his own.

They ate on a rug under the trees. Mrs. Appleby had provided a cold roast chicken with pickles, fresh-baked bread with butter wrapped in oilcloth, apples, and a liberal supply of her succulent oatmeal cakes. A jug of home-brewed beer completed the menu, and it looked so good that Margaret was persuaded to try a small glass, too.

The food tasted wonderful, and even had she not been hungry, Margaret would have been spurred to eat by Jemmy's prodigious gusto. He devoured everything the others left and still eyed the hamper with regret when it was pronounced empty at last. "I'll go down and check the *Gull*, then," he said after making sure no crumb had eluded him. And in the next moment he was bounding down the hill in great leaps.

"How can he?" wondered Margaret. "After what he has eaten."

"One of the talents of boys," replied Sir Justin. He had settled back against the trunk of one of the beeches and was reclining there contentedly, the last of the beer beside him.

"Is it?" She looked at the littered cloth. "I suppose I should tidy up."

"Not yet, surely. Look, there is a hawk."

Following his pointing finger, she saw the bird far way, floating on the wind, its wings outstretched and motionless. Suddenly it folded them and hurtled earthward, to disappear behind some trees onshore. "Oh," exclaimed Margaret softly.

"He has seen something." Keighley sipped his beer. "So, you have finished the book I gave you?"

"Yes, last night. It took me quite a time, I know."

"What did you think?"

Margaret frowned. "Well, some of the ideas seemed good, but others . . ."

"Yes?"

"They were very extreme."

He smiled a little. "Too radical?"

"I suppose they were. I could not help but think . . ."

"What?"

"Well, that the author exaggerated. I know that many people are poor, and that they lack the luxuries I have taken for granted, but I cannot believe that their situation is as bad as that book makes out." She shivered. "Some of the descriptions were dreadful."

"But very real, I assure you."

Margaret looked distressed. "In a few isolated cases, perhaps? But surely such terrible hardship is not widespread. Indeed, it cannot be—not here."

"Not here," echoed Keighley mockingly. "How do you know? Have you ever looked?"

"No, but others, those in charge of the government, must have done so. They would not allow this . . ."

"You think not?"

"*Yes.*" She glared at him; it seemed to her he was criticizing her father, who was in fact in government, by his skeptical tone.

Keighley was the victim of mixed feelings. He had made this expedition somewhat against his better judgment. His resolve to avoid Margaret or keep a distance between them was unchanged, but the temptation to get out of the inn in such a pleasant manner had been irresistible, and though he had tried to discourage her from coming, he could hardly forbid it in the face of the Applebys' urging. And once they were on the water, his spirits had been too high to quell. But now he was regretting the trip again. This conversation was reemphasizing the insidious alteration in their relationship. Whereas before he would have felt contempt and impatience at the opinions she was expressing, now he felt interest and a strong desire to convince her of the truth of his own view. His best course would be to brush off the subject and suggest they pack up for the return journey.

Having firmly decided this, he said, "I could show you that you are mistaken."

Margaret raised her eyebrows.

"In this very neighborhood, I daresay," he added.

"What do you mean?"

"Poverty is far more widespread than you know, and I can prove it."

"I'm not sure—"

"Are you afraid of the truth?" he interrupted, wondering as the words emerged if he was speaking to her or to himself.

"*No!*"

"Well, then?"

"You may show me what you please. Perhaps you will find that *you* are the one who is mistaken."

"We shall see." Having somehow committed himself to what he continued to see as a foolish course, Sir Justin rose. "We should be going back, I suppose."

Margaret looked at the view regretfully. "All right. I will put the things away if you will call Jemmy."

He started to offer to help, then thought better of it. "Very well." He walked to the edge of the hill and signaled to the boy. As Jemmy jumped up to obey his summons Keighley turned back and, to his own astonishment, heard himself say, "Whatever happened to young Manningham?"

Margaret froze, her hand poised over the basket with a soiled napkin. "Happened?"

Cursing himself for a fool, Justin struggled to find words to redeem this awkward situation. But all that came out was, "Yes."

"H-He left, I imagine."

"Left your house?"

"Yes."

"He was . . . unhappy?"

Margaret laughed harshly and shakily. "Oh, no. I would say frightened, rather. Afraid that he might somehow be forced to marry a disgraced girl and ruin his political career."

"Puppy!" As the epithet escaped him Sir Justin put a hand to his forehead. Had he gone mad? His wound must be affecting his mind for him to blurt out such idiocies. He would never have done so in the past. And yet he was amazed to find in himself a desire to take Manningham by the scruff of the neck and thrash him.

Margaret was shaking her head. "He only wanted to marry me because of my father's political connections, so he could not be expected to withstand such a blow." Her voice was extraordinarily calm; she heard it as if it were a stranger's. "I see that now. I didn't then."

Silence fell and lengthened between them. Margaret went back to putting things in the basket, unable to raise her eyes. Keighley was again silently cursing his stupidity, with an intensity that might have been directed at another as well. Both were visibly relieved when Jemmy bounded over the brow of the hill and said, "What, going already? We have hours of daylight left."

"Nonetheless, I think we should get back," replied Keighley in a tone so harsh that the boy stared.

"Yes, sir."

"Everything is ready," added Margaret in a high, unnatural voice.

"Yes, miss," said Jemmy, shouldering the basket quickly. Though not an unusually sensitive lad, even he could feel the constraint in the air. He turned and started down the hill again.

"You go ahead," said Margaret hurriedly. "I'll be along in a moment."

Sir Justin started to answer her, then closed his mouth and turned away.

12

Margaret and Sir Justin avoided each other the following day. He was still cursing himself, and she was sorely puzzled. All her worries and doubts had come flooding back during their final conversation on the island, and she was now more confused than ever about her feelings and situation. The sail home had been uncomfortably silent, leaving her ample time to wonder what had changed since the morning. She had felt both unaccountably elated and nervously unhappy, and she could see no reason for either emotion.

Yet despite this unease, it seemed a decided thing that Keighley would show Margaret what he called the true condition of the poor. Each might now have wished to postpone or even forget this promise, but neither said so. To speak of the growing constraint between them seemed impossible to Margaret and foolish to Keighley. Thus, the idea was pursued and plans made for the next day but one. Sir Justin talked to the Applebys and other villagers, and determined where to go. Margaret, when informed that all was set and asked if she remained willing, merely nodded and turned away.

They set out the following morning in the Applebys' gig. Keighley was feeling well enough to drive it, though

Jem accompanied them in case he should tire, privately thinking their expedition crack-brained. The sun had disappeared behind a screen of racing clouds today, and though it did not seem likely to rain, the atmosphere was wholly different from that on their picnic. The shifting light gave the sea an odd, metallic sheen and turned vegetation somber and dull. They drove in silence along the seawall and around to the road south of the village. Margaret was relieved to see their direction; she had feared that they might travel the route she and Keighley had taken from Devon. "Where are we going?" she asked as Sir Justin turned the gig.

"A little inland," he replied. "To some farms."

"How do you know where to go?"

"From our hosts and other villagers. The poor are usually well known in their neighborhood."

"But rare," suggested Margaret, "if we have to drive so far to find them."

"I could have shown you examples close to the inn. Not everyone in the village is as prosperous as the Applebys. But I thought it might be awkward. And I wanted you to see a more representative family. The rural poor on the land, or more often *not* on it because there is no work, are worst off today. Factory laborers endure dreadful conditions, but they are far fewer in numbers."

Curiosity overcame Margaret's uneasiness. "How do you know? How did you find out these things?"

He smiled wryly. "I did not close my eyes to them, in the first place. Any landowner can see hardship if he really looks instead of blinding himself to the truth. And then I talked to a great many people, from all classes, and read what I could find on the subject."

"You truly believe that poverty is widespread?" she responded, frowning.

"It is not a matter of belief. It is fact. I am not talking

about my *opinions* when I speak of the poor, but of real people and existing conditions."

He sounded so certain that she was shaken. She had heard over and over in her father's house that the radicals exaggerated and distorted reality, that most Englishmen were comfortable and happy, in their varying degrees. But Keighley seemed confident that he could show her the opposite. Could there be some deception involved? But how? And why? She shifted in her seat. Everything was so different now; she was so changed that she was almost prepared to find she had been deceived all her life. Abruptly she felt a wave of fear about the future. She had pushed such concerns from her mind for weeks, but now the time was coming when they must be faced. She shivered and wondered what in the world she would do.

"What is it?" asked Keighley. "Are you cold?" He was frowning down at her, for though overcast, the August day was sultry.

"No, no," said Margaret quickly.

He continued to look at her for a moment, then added, "We are nearly there, I think, aren't we, Jem?" The boy signified that they were. "Have you changed your mind? Do you wish to go back?"

"Not at all." Margaret straightened. He would not fob her off so easily.

He nodded and turned his attention back to the horse. In a short while they left the road for a rutted lane and soon reached a small stone cottage. Keighley pulled up and helped Margaret down. "This is the home of the Jones family," he told her. "Mr. Jones, his wife, and the elder children work in the fields, so they will not be here."

"But should we . . ."

Sir Justin was not listening to her. He had walked to the cottage door and knocked. After a prolonged interval the door opened slowly, and a small girl peered around its panels. "Good day," said Keighley, offering her a sovereign.

The child, who could not have been more than six, stared at the coin with awe. She did not reach for it.

"This is for you," urged Sir Justin. "The lady is thirsty. May we have a drink of water?"

The girl gazed up at him, her round eyes painfully large in a pinched face. "Thirsty?" she repeated in a thick dialect.

"Yes. May we have a little water?" He again extended the coin to her.

Slowly her hand came around the door. Keighley handed her the sovereign as Margaret thought that she had never seen so thin an arm. The child held the money reverently in a cupped palm, then, with a furtive glance at them, swiftly bit it to see if it was real. Discovering real gold, she was struck dumb.

"May we have a glass of water?" said Sir Justin again.

The little girl edged backward, opening the door as she went. With an unobtrusive signal, Keighley indicated that Margaret should approach, and they entered the low doorway together.

The room was dim, and at first Margaret could see nothing. But as her eyes adjusted she realized that the floor was packed earth and the walls whitewashed stone, blackened by smoke and grime. There was a fireplace on the back wall but no fire. A long table stood before it and, with three broken-down chairs, constituted the furniture in the visible part of the house. A dingy curtain closed off about a third of the space, and Margaret supposed that was the bedroom. Under her gaze the curtain seemed to shiver, then pulled back to reveal a tiny, half-clad boy and, behind him, a large bed containing three even smaller children. These gazed with wide-eyed fright over the top of one thin blanket.

"What you want?" asked the little boy with a piteous attempt at ferocity.

"Shh, Dan'l," said the girl who had greeted them. She had gone to the table and now returned with a tin dipper of water.

Keighley took it and turned to Margaret, shutting off the children with his broad back. "Pretend to drink," he murmured. "Do not touch it with your lips."

Confused, she did so, and he handed the dipper back. The girl eyed it, then turned to put it back.

"Thank you," said Keighley. "Your mother and father are in the fields, I suppose?"

Both children gazed at him with stony suspicion.

"And your older brothers and sisters? How many of them?"

They made no answer.

With a shrug, he turned away. "They will not talk to us alone. We had best be going on."

Biting her lower lip, Margaret gazed about her. Could many people live this way, crowded together with not one beautiful thing in their house? Fumbling in her reticule, she found another sovereign. "Here," she stammered, pressing it on the boy clutching the curtain.

He glared.

"Take it."

Grudgingly he allowed her to give him the coin.

"Come," said Keighley gently. He put a hand under her elbow and led her out of the cottage. The door shut firmly behind them.

"That is a relatively prosperous laborer's household," he added when they were under way once more. "Both parents have work, along with some older children. How many? Do you know, Jem?"

He shrugged. "Three or four."

"Ah. So, you see, the family has quite a large income,

with so many earning. Many live on much less, and when there is no work to be had, they starve."

"Less," murmured Margaret, horrified. "But they have *nothing*."

"On the contrary, they have a dry cottage, some furniture and clothing, and a supply of fuel. Did you notice the shed? They are comparatively well off. We are going to see a family that is considerably less so."

"B-But the children . . . they were so thin, and frightened of us."

"Yes."

"How can you call them well off?"

"I said 'comparatively.'"

"And why were they not out playing or . . . or something?"

"I daresay they are told to stay inside, and they probably do not get enough food to make them energetic."

"How can you speak so coldly?" cried Margaret, appalled at his matter-of-factness. "Those were little children."

"I know they were," he replied quietly. "If you had seen as many worse cases as I, you would speak as I do. But my tone does not mean I accept such things as right."

She gazed up at him, half incredulous, half pleading. "There cannot be many so . . ."

"Millions."

She shook her head, as if to rid it of the vision.

"I am sorry to distress you, but for every wealthy child who has all the luxuries and an abundance of spirits, there are twenty of those we just saw, or worse. Most commonly worse. In the cities they can steal, but even that does not get them enough to eat."

"I cannot believe it. I . . . I *won't*."

Keighley did not reply. He knew that tone too well. It meant that she was beginning, in fact, to believe, and hated the process. He felt suddenly sad. Perhaps he had been wrong to bring her. Did she really need to know the truth? The knowledge was painful, and he hated to see her suffer. But another part of him stubbornly insisted that she must. It was somehow important that she be able to judge the right of this question, important to him. With an impatient flick of the reins, he banished this dangerous train of thought. "We are going next to the house of an unemployed laborer," he said rather harshly. "There you will see *real* hardship."

In the next hour Margaret was shocked as she had never been in her life. Words that she had glibly used or heard unfeeling—poverty, hunger, bitterness—became hauntingly real, and she knew she would never be rid of the scenes she had witnessed as Keighley talked to three out-of-work laborers and their wives. She herself had not the knowledge or the courage to say much, but she listened and looked and engraved the exchanges on her memory. Even later, when they were driving back toward the Red Lion, she could still see it all, particularly the eyes of the men as they talked about trying to get work. They had burned with a daunting combination of iron will, hope, and anger that had made Margaret feel insignificant and worthless. And all of them had agreed with Keighley's opinion that their plight was widespread. Each knew many others in his own situation.

She felt beaten by their emotions and drained of her own. As they went slowly home she could not speak. She knew that if she tried, she would cry, and she did not want to give Keighley that satisfaction. No doubt he was gloating beside her—she dared not look up—at the triumph of his point of view over hers.

Margaret could not know that he had seen this happen over and over, beginning with himself and continuing with various friends and political allies to whom he had shown the same things. He knew precisely what she was feeling, and pitied her sincerely. He also knew better than to speak.

Despite her turmoil, Margaret found the journey back short. It seemed only a moment before Jem was jumping down and going to the horse's head to lead him back into his stable. Keighley handed her down from the gig and offered his arm. She bent her head under her bonnet brim and took it, wanting only to escape to her own room and recover.

"Are you all right?" he asked as they walked.

Margaret nodded silently.

"I doubt it. You know . . ."

"You were right, you were right," cried the girl. "There, I have admitted it, and you needn't tell me so in your odiously superior way. I cannot help it that I was never told . . . never shown . . ." She broke off abruptly, swallowing tears that she would not let him see.

"Of course you were not. And I was certainly not going to taunt you with it. What do you think me? I have experienced exactly what you are feeling now. My father took me on just such a tour when I was ten years old. And I have since exposed others. I know how hard it is."

Margaret looked up. "Ten?"

He smiled wryly. "Indeed. It was just before I went to school. He determined that I should see something of the real world around me before I was 'spoiled' by Eton. He had not wanted me to go to school at all, but Mama insisted. I was deeply shocked. I don't believe I said a word during the first two weeks of term. My housemaster was about to write my parents when I finally opened my mouth, and then he wrote because what came out was rank, radical heresy. Of course Papa's reply shocked him nearly as much."

Margaret smiled slightly.

"It is hard to accept. It will take time. You should not expect to feel just as usual after this morning."

This brought back her tremulousness. "It was the children I couldn't bear."

He nodded. "I know."

"They looked so hopeless." To her chagrin, Margaret started to cry.

Keighley stopped, and she pulled her arm from his. She was angry at herself for breaking down, but she could not seem to stop. She groped for a handkerchief in her reticule and applied it to her streaming eyes. If only he would just go on and leave her.

This actually occurred to him, but he rejected the idea as callous. It was because of him that she was crying; he could not simply abandon her. But what ought he to do? He had dealt with numerous sobbing females in his life, but never in these circumstances. The usual solution—to offer a supporting shoulder—was unsuitable for a variety of reasons. He had never before taken a young girl on a tour such as today's, and he vowed never to do so again.

From behind her handkerchief Margaret sobbed, "Leave me alone. Go away." But her voice was too muffled to be intelligible. When he did not go, she looked up, her eyes brimming and reproachful, and met his.

This was too much. Without further thought, he put his arms around her and pulled her against his chest, one hand in her blond curls. "Go on and cry," he said. "It helps."

Margaret was at first so startled that she nearly stopped crying. It was so odd to find her cheek resting on his lapel and her shivering frame enclosed in strong arms. She felt him stroke her hair, and suddenly it seemed that there was even more to cry about than she had imagined. She abandoned herself wholly to tears.

It was some time before this emotional storm passed. Margaret sobbed, and Sir Justin held her firmly. At last she began gradually to regain control, and both of them came to their senses abruptly a moment later. Margaret stiffened and sniffed desperately. Keighley immediately dropped his arms and stepped back in dismay, wishing savagely that he had obeyed his baser impulses and left her.

Seeing his face, Margaret gulped back another sob. "I . . . I'm sorry," she said foolishly.

"On the contrary. It is I who must beg your pardon," was the stiff reply. "Your distress led me to overstep the bounds of propriety, and I hope you will believe that compassion was my only motive."

This phrasing was so unlike him that Margaret could only swallow again and nod.

"It might be best if I left you now. Unless I can be of some help?"

She shook her head vehemently, desperate to be alone with her chaotic thoughts.

He bowed slightly and turned away. Margaret watched him stride along the street and around the corner, then turned her attention to composing herself enough to reach her bedchamber unremarked.

13

A frosty atmosphere descended upon the Red Lion and did not lift through two long days. Keighley, pronounced much improved, was allowed to go out alone for the first time, so now it was he who walked along the shore and Margaret who stayed in her room. She ventured out only for meals, and even then said and ate little. Some of the rosy color she had gained faded, and her shoulders showed the beginning of their old droop.

These outward signs were merely suggestive of her inner turmoil, which was far more intense. During the long, quiet hours in her room Margaret endlessly reviewed the events that had brought her here and the actions she had taken. She could not see what she could have done differently, but she wished with all her heart that things had not gone as they had. For Margaret had never been so uneasy and unhappy in her life. Something had happened to her in the last week, something she did not at all understand, and it now seemed to her that the future offered nothing but dreary routine and loneliness.

She had resisted thinking about what she would do for as long as possible, but now, somehow, worries intruded, and she felt obliged to plan. She tried to imagine herself going on to Penzance or some other town and finding work as she had once thought to do. The vision nearly made her weep. But when she considered returning to her parents, this alternative seemed even worse. No future looked pleasant or possible, and she could not understand how this had come to be. She had always known it would not be easy to make her own way. But why had it suddenly become impossible to contemplate?

At this stage in her meditations the image of Sir Justin Keighley usually intruded, most particularly the look on his face when he had backed away from her after their embrace. Margaret always shuddered when she thought of it and immediately forced her thoughts elsewhere. She would not think of *that*, though she refused to wonder why it was so painful or why the question of her future suddenly seemed so important.

Keighley himself had a rather clearer understanding of the situation, but that did not make him any happier. On his long walks he also pondered the future and his own mental state, coming to some hard conclusions. He had known for some time that his feelings were getting out of control, and when he had, much against his better judgment and even his will, taken Margaret in his arms, warnings had sounded throughout his brain. The fact that he found holding her slender frame and stroking her silken hair very pleasant simply intensified his determination to stop.

He had heard many stories of attachments fostered by isolation and propinquity. Matchmaking mamas often counted on it, and freedom-loving bachelors frequently lamented a month spent at the country place of such a parent—a month that ended in an offer and an announcement in the *Morning Post*. He knew of such a case himself, one of the most blatantly unhappy marriages in the *ton*.

Thus, he was not about to be caught so. He had, he told himself, responded naturally to the unfortunate circumstance of remaining alone with a reasonably attractive young lady for a period of weeks. That this young lady had nursed him kindly and shown a gratifying susceptibility to his influence in the matter of politics had, of course, aided the process. But it was no more than that. There was no question of deep feelings or marriage. Keighley's lips always hardened into a determined line as he thought this.

His course now was clear. He must extricate himself from the situation with as much grace and consideration as possible, the former necessity far outweighing the latter. If the girl cut up rough . . . Here his thoughts jibed. Why should she? She had hated the idea of marrying him enough to run away from home.

No, he must prepare to leave this place; that was the best solution. She could do as she pleased. He would help, of course, with money or advice, but she was not his responsibility after all. His shoulder was feeling nearly fit, and he must make plans to depart.

He came to this conclusion on the morning following Margaret's tears, but, curiously, he did nothing about it that day or the next. He told himself that to hurry the matter would be a clear insult and that he must smooth things over before he left, yet he made no move to do so. The two met at dinner, made some slight, stiff conversation, and parted again, neither venturing to communicate his thoughts, and the air of the Red Lion seemed to grow heavier and heavier with tension.

Waking on the third morning, Margaret suddenly found she could stand it no longer. If she sat one more hour in the inn, she thought, she would begin to scream with vexation. She must get out, but she did not want to meet Keighley along the beach. Out of nowhere the face of Mrs. Dowling came before her. She had not seen the old woman for some time. She would go to call on her.

With this decision came a sudden desire to confide.

Margaret dressed hurriedly and ate her breakfast without knowing what it was. A desperate wish for help was building in her, but did she dare give in to it with Mrs. Dowling? And if she did, risking exposure, would it do any good?

She found Mrs. Dowling at home, tending a great steaming kettle over the fire. For a moment after she entered the cottage her initial vision of the woman recurred. Stirring the boiling pot, Mrs. Dowling did look a great deal like a fairy-tale witch. But the illusion was broken when she pointed her long-handled spoon and said, "Blackberry jam. The berries is fine this year."

With a smile at her own silliness, Margaret sat down in the windowseat and wondered what to say. Should she ask advice, and, if so, where should she begin? "How is your daughter?" she ventured finally.

Mrs. Dowling looked gratified. "Carrie? She's well. Her oldest son is getting married next week, and she's ever so busy with that."

"Really? So you will be a great-grandmother soon."

Mrs. Dowling chuckled. "Bless you, I am that. My son in Plymouth married his daughter three years ago, and she has a girl of her own now, a strapping little lass."

"How strange it must be."

Mrs. Dowling peered at her through the blackberry steam. "Strange, miss?"

"To have grandchildren and great-grandchildren. I can hardly imagine it."

"It's not so strange. Or, if it be, the strangeness bain't in *you*, if you see what I mean. I feel the same as I did when my children was small. If it weren't for mirrors, I'd swear I *was* the same. It's the world that changes."

Margaret pondered. "I don't know. I feel very different lately."

The old woman chuckled again. "You're young yet, miss. Wait ten years and then see."

Margaret sighed. Where would she be in ten years, and doing what? For a moment she envied Mrs. Dowling, who had probably never had to wonder such a thing in her life.

"You're looking sad, dearie," commented the woman. "Be it your 'brother'?"

The way she spoke this final word made Margaret look up sharply, then slump. She tried to decide logically what she should do, but she was not feeling logical. "You're right," she said finally. "He isn't my brother."

"Ah?"

"He isn't even related to me." And, in a sudden rush, the whole story came pouring out: the dinner party and its aftermath, her parents' reaction and her own, the flight and pursuit—everything. She spoke quickly and none too coherently, but Mrs. Dowling seemed to take it all in, nodding sagely at intervals. When at last she was done, Margaret sank back in the windowseat with a great sigh. She felt an immense relief at having told someone the truth, and a tremulous hope that this might somehow make it all right.

"What I don't see," said Mrs. Dowling, "is why you were so set against marrying him. He seems a likely gentleman."

"Well, you see," began Margaret, "I . . ." She stopped, remembering clearly what she had though of Keighley at that time. She could have recited a detailed list of his faults and heresies. *Now*, however, these all seemed nonsense to her. His political opinions were radical—but they had a rightness about which one could care. His personal habits and behavior had shown none of the depravity she had been led to expect. He had had more thought for propriety than she, and in spite of his brusqueness, he had been patient with her, even kind. In fact, she realized, she was convinced that her mother had been utterly mistaken about the man, if not deliberately malicious.

Mrs. Dowling had been watching her face. Now she looked inquiring.

"I . . . I thought I had good reasons," stammered Margaret.

"And now you don't think so?"

"No . . . That is, it does not matter in the least what I think. There is no question of marriage any longer."

"No?"

"No. I told you we settled all that at once." A memory of resting in Keighley's arms swept suddenly over her, and Margaret trembled.

"Seems to me that might have changed," suggested Mrs. Dowling. "Jem Appleby claims you had a fine time out in the *Gull* last week. Said he thought you were sweet on each other."

"That's . . . nonsense. He is just a boy. He misunderstood."

"Happen he did." The old woman kept her eyes on Margaret's face. "Happen not. But why tell me all this, miss?"

"What?"

Mrs. Dowling merely watched her. Margaret avoided her eyes. There was a short silence, then the girl added, "I am very confused."

The other nodded.

"We *did* have a good time on the picnic at first, and . . . and then . . ." She hesitated, then, with a sensation like shutting her eyes and plunging into a cold bath, she told Mrs. Dowling about their expedition in the neighborhood and its aftermath. "We have hardly spoken since," she finished. "And I . . . I don't know what to *do*."

Mrs. Dowling put down her spoon, pulled the kettle farther from the fire, and wiped her hands on her apron. She appeared to be thinking hard. "How do you *feel*?" she asked finally. "About the gentleman."

"I don't know. Confused. Uneasy. Rather . . . frightened." As she said this last Margaret frowned. What did *that* mean?

The old woman nodded slowly. She came to sit opposite Margaret in the windowseat and look directly into her eyes. "You and the gentleman must have a talk," she said. "You've been acting like a pair of mooning children, and you'd best stop it. Why, my Carrie would have known better when she was fifteen."

"I . . . I don't understand."

"No, you don't. It's a scandal the way they rear you young ladies—filling your head with books and foreign talk and such, and never letting you learn what comes natural. My Carrie . . . Well, you don't care for that." She appeared to ponder again. "You go to your gentleman, straight, and ask him what he means to do."

"Do?"

"About him and you."

"About . . ."

"Lord, child, it's plain you're mad for each other. And he's as noddy as you. You must *tell* him so."

"Mad for . . . oh, no! You've made a mistake. It's nothing like that."

Mrs. Dowling shrugged and rose to reclaim her spoon.

"It *isn't*," insisted Margaret.

The woman pushed the kettle back over the fire and began to stir the jam.

Margaret jumped up. "I am sorry I came. I hope you will keep your word and not tell anyone what I said?"

"Aye."

"Thank you. I . . . please pay no attention to the things I mentioned. They aren't of the least consequence."

Mrs. Dowling shrugged again.

"Good day."

The old woman nodded. Margaret hesitated, then turned and left the cottage.

She fled almost blindly down the village lanes to the seawall and clung to it for a moment, staring out to sea. Huge white clouds drifted across the sky, casting moving shadows on low waves. Recalling that she was likely to encounter Keighley here, she ran along the lane to the steps leading to the beach and was soon crouched by the pool in her old place. Hidden by the foliage there, she put her head in her arms and gave herself up to confusion.

It was nearly half an hour before she straightened again and took several deep breaths. The sound of trickling water in the quiet had soothed her, and she felt more able to think. Though it was nearly time for luncheon, she did not move. She wasn't hungry.

Mrs. Dowling's words echoed in her head. The idea was totally ridiculous, of course, but why, then, did it arouse such violent emotions? She should laugh, Margaret thought, at the mere suggestion that she and Keighley were "mad for" each other; instead she trembled with . . . with what? It could not be fear. She knew that she no longer harbored her misguided terror of the man.

Painstakingly she went back over everything that had occurred between them, from the beginning, and examined her reactions in each case. When she came to his embrace, she started to tremble violently again, and this time it was clear that it was due to a combination of excitement and uncertainty. She had enjoyed that closeness, she admitted, and she longed to know if Keighley felt the same.

His expression as he drew away from her rose vividly before her again. He had *not* enjoyed it. He had been appalled; it was only too obvious. And Margaret now realized that her response to his hurried withdrawal had been disappointment and chagrin. She had wanted to remain in his arms, to discover more about the new sensations wakening in her body.

Rubbing her eyes with one hand, Margaret gave in. Mrs. Dowling was right. Somehow, ironically, she had fallen in love with Justin Keighley. How her mother would gloat over that. But he had not been subject to the same capricious fate. He saw her precisely as he always had, as a tiresome problem that must be solved.

For some time Margaret felt sorry for herself. It seemed so terribly unfair that she should suffer unrequited love for a man she had once fled in disgust. And that he should be absolutely unaffected. Mrs. Dowling had said that one remained the same while the world changed, but Margaret felt exactly the opposite. She had changed beyond recognition, but the world continued unaltered.

When she had brought herself close to tears with these lugubrious ruminations, Margaret suddenly remembered another kind of moment—during their picnic when Keighley asked about Philip Manningham. And with that recollection came a number of others. She chewed her thumbnail and reviewed them. Was it possible that Sir Justin was not so oblivious as he might wish? Could he have been appalled not by their embrace but by his own feelings during it? Margaret hardly dared hope, but more and more memories came now to support that conclusion. She could easily believe that Sir Justin would resist falling in love with her, for a variety of reasons. She had done the same herself. But if he was doing so, and was not simply indifferent, he must be made to stop.

With this thought, Margaret rose and began pacing beside her pool. Once she would have been too diffident to contemplate what now ran through her mind, but that seemed years ago. If there was the least chance of success, she was ready to fight for what she wanted. Sir Justin could refuse to love her, but he could not do so without facing her and saying it. And she had the feeling that denial would be difficult in those circumstances. Margaret smiled. If he thought he could simply continue to avoid her, and then slip away without ever having dealt with this question, he was quite wrong.

Resolved, she shook out her skirts and started to walk back toward the Red Lion. How was her plan best accomplished? she wondered. Keighley was probably out now, and in any case she did not feel ready to face him *yet*. She would wait until the evening. Yes. They met automatically at dinner; she would do it then. And perhaps there were some steps she could take to make it easier.

She smiled again—a smile that her mother would have found alarmingly alien—and tossed her head. She saw how it could be managed. It would be wholly unexpected, too, and that was a great advantage. She took a little skipping step and bounded up the seawall steps. Tonight could be glorious, but there was much to do first.

14

After making certain arrangements with Mrs. Appleby, Margaret returned to her bedchamber and took stock. The dinner would be good—Sir Justin approved of Mrs. Appleby's cooking—so she need concern herself only with her own appearance. But this was not an insignificant problem. She was heartily sick of the three gowns she had brought, and though she had not thought much about it before, she now realized that her efforts at hairdressing left much to be desired. Even after all this time she had still not become as skilled as her maid at home.

A small mirror hung above her washstand, and she went to peer into it. She could hardly see anything. Margaret stood back. There was a much larger glass in Keighley's room, she knew. Did she dare try to bring it here? He was probably out, but how could she be sure? She did not want to meet him before she was ready.

Going to the door, she opened it a crack and listened. Though there were sounds of activity downstairs, the first floor of the inn was silent and Keighley's bedroom door was open. He must be out. Margaret slipped into the hall and moved quietly down it, stopping to listen again at intervals. When she reached Keighley's chamber, she paused, then slowly peered around the corner to make sure it was empty. Yes. She hurried in, picked up the full-length mirror that stood on oak legs in the corner, and lugged it out to the corridor. It was heavier than she had expected, and she had to put it down for a moment there. But she waited only to catch her breath before trying again, with a better grip. It was awkward, but she could manage it.

She was almost to her own room when a deep voice from the direction of the stairs said, "Can I help, miss?"

Margaret nearly dropped the mirror; she craned her neck to find Mr. Appleby standing on the landing and looking through the stair rail at her. He seemed puzzled. "I . . . I wanted to use this mirror," she gasped. "The one in my room is so small."

The innkeeper came up the remaining steps. "To be sure it is, miss. We should have thought. Mr. Camden doesn't use that glass, and a young lady is likely to want one. Let me take it for you." He lifted the mirror easily and carried it into Margaret's room. "I'll set it right here in the corner, under the window."

"Thank you."

"And shall I take the small one to the other bedroom? I reckon your brother can use it for shaving."

"Yes, but don't mention that I . . . I mean . . . he teases me so about being vain."

Appleby grinned. "I won't say a word, miss. Or, if he asks, I'll say the wife decided to move the furniture about. She often does."

Margaret could not help returning his smile. "Thank you."

Nodding, he went out. "You must tell us when there's something you'd like, miss. We're only too happy."

Thanking him again, Margaret shut the door and sank down on her bed. Her heart was still hammering. When Appleby had first spoken, she had been sure it was

Keighley. Now she took several deep breaths and gradually calmed. All this fuss over a mirror.

After a while she rose and went to look at herself. This glass was good—she could see her whole figure—and the reflection it gave back startled Margaret considerably. She had known her appearance had changed. The fit of her dresses and her small mirror had told her that. But she had not quite realized the extent of the alteration until now. She turned this way and that, surveying herself from all angles. Not only was her figure fuller and more rounded, but her shoulders were straighter and she moved differently. She could not decide just how. There was a new springiness in her step and fluidity in her motion. Her face looked different, too. It was slightly fuller, so that her eyes no longer seemed too large for it, and her formerly pale cheeks glowed with color. But her hair—Margaret put a hand to the fine blond curls—that was much the same. Something must be done there.

Her gaze shifted to her white muslin gown, and she made a wry face. She never wished to see this dress again, or the blue or the pink, but she would have to wear one of them tonight. She took the other two from the wardrobe and held them up one by one before her. It hardly mattered, but she supposed the pink looked best.

There was a tap on her door, and one of the younger Appleby girls called, "Miss? I've filled the bath as you wanted."

"Thank you." Putting the dresses on the bed, Margaret gathered her things and went to have a hot bath, thinking that at least some luxuries remained to her.

At six she stood before the long mirror once again, checking her appearance one last time before going downstairs. It was still quite light, but she had also lit two candles to see the effect. The pink dress was all right; it was clean, at least, and fit her better than it ever had. The plain, round-necked bodice and puffed sleeves set off her newly rounded arms and shoulders, and the color intensified hers. But Margaret's main attention was to her hair. She had worked on it for nearly an hour, and she was pleased with the results. She had gathered it in a knot on top of her head, with curls falling over her ears and forehead. It was a style she had never worn before, and she thought it became her.

She had also, for the first time, opened the little casket of jewelry she had packed, which had miraculously survived its accident on the road and subsequent rescue. Most things, like her pearls did not suit the dress or the occasion—she did not want to alert Keighley to her purpose—but she had brought a pair of tiny silver earrings ornamented with a single drop of opal, and these she fastened in her ears. They caught the candlelight beautifully and, she thought, gave her head a much more elegant appearance.

Margaret took a breath, shook out her skirts, and snuffed the candles. She was ready. She had heard Sir Justin go down a few minutes before, and she followed him with a beating heart but, she hoped, an impassive expression.

He awaited her in the back parlor, where the table was set as usual for dinner. He was sitting in an armchair reading a newspaper, a habit he had taken up in the last few days, and she did not attempt to interrupt but merely said good evening and sat down. A few minutes later Annie Appleby came in with a steaming crock of soup, and they began to eat.

"Did you have a pleasant day?" asked Margaret.

"Yes, thank you."

"You went walking?"

"Along the shore, yes." He looked directly at her for the first time that evening, his expression showing puzzlement. Margaret had not been talking much in the last two days, and something else, which he could not pin down, seemed different.

"It was a lovely day for it. I was out also for a while."

He nodded as Annie removed the soup plates and set down fresh crockery. She served them both with roast chicken, new potatoes, and fresh peas, then went out. Keighley began to eat, only to pause in surprise when the girl returned with a bottle of wine and poured out two glasses. "What's this?" he asked.

Margaret smiled. "Mrs. Appleby thought we should celebrate, since you are so much better." This was not strictly true. The wine had been Margaret's suggestion and rather difficult to procure, but Mrs. Appleby was primed to support her if necessary.

"I see."

She picked up her glass, hoping that her almost complete inexperience of wine did not show, and said, "To your continued health," sipping a little.

Keighley raised one black eyebrow but drank. "Thank you. And, speaking of my health, it is so much improved that we should think of leaving here."

"Yes," replied Margaret agreeably. "You must get back to your estate. I daresay they have been worried about you."

"I sent a letter yesterday. Jem carried it to Falmouth, to a trustworthy man he knows there. It should reach my butler without revealing our direction."

She swallowed a bite of chicken that had nearly choked her. "Ah. You did not tell me." Things were not going exactly as she had planned.

"No." Keighley drank more wine. He felt he should have told her, but he had not been able to find a time that seemed good. Indeed, now that he had raised the subject of leaving, he wished he hadn't. Why had he felt compelled to ruin their dinner when Margaret was looking so . . . Harshly cutting off this errant thought, he added, "We might think of going at the end of the week."

Margaret nodded absently, causing Sir Justin to clutch the stem of his wineglass so tightly his knuckles whitened. She noticed his reaction with joy.

"Where do you intend to go?" he asked.

She smiled and shrugged slightly, watching his eyes.

"You do not mean to tell me?"

"After all, it can be no concern of yours."

"No concern?" he began hotly, but Annie returned just then with a dish of pudding and set it on the table.

"Will there be anything else?" she asked.

"No," snapped Keighley, and the girl went out with a startled glance at him over her shoulder. "Now, listen to me," he continued.

Margaret interrupted him. "You know, I have been thinking a good deal since our visit to those people."

Sir Justin stiffened. Was the girl about to throw his behavior in his face? That would get her nowhere.

"And reading, too," she added, which was true. She had spent two hours with the book on reform that afternoon. "I find my opinions are greatly changed."

This was not what he had expected. "Do you?"

"Yes. Since I have seen how people really live, I agree with many of the proposals in the book you lent me. You know that I thought them extreme at first. Now I don't."

He merely watched her, bemused.

"It seems to me that half measures are dreadful. They raise people's hopes but accomplish so little."

"That may be true. But they can be gotten through, and at least that little accomplished. If one insists upon sweeping reform, nothing is done."

"Yes, I see. But it is so hard to think of those families we saw, and the others you tell me are all over England. They will not be affected by small reforms. They will continue to suffer." She gazed intensely into his eyes.

"That is one of the infuriating things about politics," he agreed, meeting her eyes. "I found it nearly insupportable when I first began. But gradually one comes to see that one must simply do what one can. Sulking over impossibilities helps no one." He smiled a little. "I know. I did it for a year when I was twenty."

Margaret sternly controlled her answering smile. She did not want to interrupt a process that was going so well. "It is the children I cannot forget," she went on. "I pity the adults, of course, but the children could do so much if they had the opportunity."

Margaret leaned forward again, bringing her face closer to his across the table, and added, "I want so to help, you see. For the last two days I have thought and thought what I might do. But I feel so powerless. I cannot stand for Parliament or make speeches or influence those who run the government. No one would listen to me. Yet I must do something. I cannot remain idle after what you have shown me."

"I believe you are serious," replied Sir Justin, his eyes on hers.

"I am. Completely." And, indeed, Margaret was not fabricating this part of her appeal. She had felt an impulse to help the people she had seen, and she would do so if a way was offered.

Keighley's hazel eyes softened. "There are things you can do. For example, a friend of mine, Lady Noonham, has started a series of charity schools for the children of laborers, particularly in the North, where the factories are increasing every day. They are educated so that they can do better than their parents."

"That is a splendid idea," exclaimed Margaret sincerely.

"She is always looking for contributions."

"Money, you mean?"

"Yes. There is never enough for such work."

"Well, I would be happy to give her whatever I can, but I want to do something *myself*."

Keighley looked puzzled.

"I want to see the people, to be with those children . . . and to work with them myself." As she spoke Margaret realized that her words were no more than the truth. The children she had seen haunted her, particularly the first little girl and boy. She could still see their eyes, shadowed by fear and ignorance, very clearly.

"You don't know what you're proposing," answered Sir Justin. "You have had a small taste of dirt and poverty, but that is quite different from facing it often or in larger concentrations, such as one finds in London."

"I know it must be. And perhaps I should not be able to endure it and would fail. But I am determined to try " Looking down, and partly forgetting her purpose tonight, Margaret repeated, "Determined. I will find a means." It suddenly occurred to her that here was a focus for her future. Whatever happened, she would retain this interest, and it would sustain and fire her. She raised her head and met Keighley's dark eyes with a new light in her own. She had set out to do one thing this evening and, in the process, discovered another.

"I believe you will," he said, impressed. His hand moved involuntarily to cover hers on the table; he was entranced by the fire and spirit that illuminated her as she spoke.

Though she pretended not to notice, Margaret's heart began to pound. "What a feeling it must be, to really help."

"I have been told so."

"But you have felt it. You have worked for the same cause."

He shrugged. "With Members of Parliament, factory owners, the Prince. It is all talk and most often useless."

"I don't believe that for an instant."

He smiled wryly. "Well, it is hardly as satisfying as what you propose."

"Indeed not, and it must therefore be all the harder. I could never keep up such a thankless struggle, and I admire you for being able to. I daresay you will be the one who makes real reform possible one day."

"We are working on a bill . . ." He broke off with a short laugh. "But you are merely being polite."

"I am not! I do admire your work. It must require immense patience and will. You fight for what you believe in. What more could anyone do?"

His grip on her hand tightened, and his eyes showed a sudden vulnerability. It was seldom he heard words like these. Most of his acquaintances and even friends mocked or criticized his efforts.

"I only hope I can be like you," she added.

"You exaggerate."

"I don't think so," she said softly. She had seen the look in his eyes, and been deeply touched by it. "I think perhaps you are the most admirable man I know." Slowly she stood and moved around the table, leaving her hand in his. When she stood beside him, she said, "Thank you for showing me . . . everything."

He gazed up at her and, in one blinding instant, saw that what he had been fighting for the past week was not the mere influence of propinquity but something much stronger and more permanent. He also stood, towering over her. "You have shown me a good deal as well."

Margaret smiled. "Have I? I can't imagine what."

"Can't you?" He released her hand and slid his arms about her waist, unsure how she would respond. A tiny part of him shrilled one last warning, which he rejected with disdain. "Can't you, indeed?"

Her heart beating wildly, Margaret put one hand on his upper arm, then the other. As he pulled her slowly closer to him she moved her hands up and around his neck. She was trembling. It was the oddest sensation to tilt her lips gradually toward his, both like and unlike the other time he had held her.

Sir Justin bent his head and kissed her, softly and lightly. His arms tightened, and he did it again, more passionately. Margaret, astonished by a flood of powerful new feelings, pressed her body against his. She felt as if her bones were melting. They kissed a third time, and Margaret's last hesitancy disappeared in the heat of their embrace. Keighley's hands wandered up her back and then down in a lingering caress, and with an answering passion.

At last he raised his head again and looked at her.

"Oh, my," breathed Margaret.

He laughed. "May I take that as a favorable judgment?"

She nodded, wide-eyed. "It is just so new to me, you know."

A flicker of concern passed over his face. "I should not have—"

"Can we try it again?" she interrupted, pulling a little at his neck.

He laughed again. "I doubt that that is wise."

"Oh, wise." Margaret was contemptuous. "All my life I did what was wise and proper. Until I met you, that is. I like the new way *much* better."

Their eyes met in a warm smile, and he bent to kiss her a fourth time.

Margaret was just giving herself up wholly to the embrace when the parlor door burst open so violently that it slammed back against the wall. "*So,*" shouted the man who stood in the opening. "Just as I expected. *Blackguard. Villain. Ravisher.*" He turned his head a little. "And you—baggage—where are your principles, your moral scruples, that I find you so?"

They had separated at the first sound. Now Margaret put a hand to her mouth. "Papa," she gasped.

15

The shouting lasted nearly an hour, accomplishing nothing. First Mr. Mayfield shouted, then Margaret, goaded by his unfair accusations, joined him, and finally Sir Justin could contain himself no longer and added his voice to theirs. They none of them listened to one another, and it was only when they became aware of the astonished faces of the Appleby family in the corridor outside the parlor that they quieted a bit.

"I shall require a room for the night," Mr. Mayfield told his hosts. "That is all. You needn't gape."

"Th-This is my father," put in Margaret.

"Aye," agreed Mr. Appleby. "We gathered as much. And *not* the gentleman's father, I take it?"

"N-No."

"I was adopted," suggested Keighley. Margaret was so startled she almost giggled. The Applebys looked unimpressed.

"Get out, get out," exclaimed Mayfield impatiently, moving to shut the door. "We'll ring if we want anything."

"There is no need to be so rude, Father," said Margaret when the door was closed. "The Applebys have been very good to us . . . to me, I mean."

"*Rude?* If you think I can bother with politeness

at a moment like this . . ." He paused to catch his breath.

"Perhaps I should leave the two of you to talk?" offered Keighley. Both Margaret and Mr. Mayfield stared at him, Mayfield with outrage and Margaret with puzzlement. The truth was that Sir Justin felt the need for a respite, a moment to think before he confronted the situation. When neither answered him, he nodded briefly and left the room.

"Well," breathed Mayfield.

"Father, what are you doing here?" Margaret was more angry than chagrined at her father's arrival and his wild accusations. Things had been going wonderfully until he came, and now all was confusion again.

"How can you ask me that? My only daughter runs away from my home—"

"And you *let* her. Leaving her to make her way as best she can for weeks."

"That was not my idea. I wished to go after you at once. Your mother . . . Well, that is by the by. In any case, once I began to search, it was by no means easy to find you."

"How did you?"

"I searched and inquired in Penzance and then in other towns thereabouts. A doctor in Falmouth finally gave me news of you."

"Ah. Dr. Brice. I am not surprised."

"Are you not, indeed? And I suppose you are also unmoved by the fact that we have been worrying about you for weeks? Your mother is prostrate. You could not spare a moment to send us word, I suppose, here in your love nest?"

"Oh, take a damper, Papa," answered Margaret impatiently.

Mr. Mayfield gaped at her like a beached fish.

"In the first place, it is not a 'love nest.' What a

ridiculous idea. We are here only while Sir Justin recovers from his wound. And in the second place, I did not send word because I did not think you wished to hear and because I did not want you descending upon me—as you *have* done."

"Did not . . ."

"You made no effort to help or understand me when I asked it, Papa. Why should I have turned to you?"

"What has happened to you, Margaret? You are . . . so different. *He* has corrupted you."

"Nonsense!"

Mr. Mayfield gaped again. His daughter had never spoken to him in this tone and had certainly never labeled anything he chose to say to her as nonsense.

"Nothing in particular has happened to me except perhaps that I have grown up a bit. I have merely been staying in this inn helping to nurse Sir Justin. He is nearly well now, and—"

"What was the matter with Keighley? How was he wounded? Dr. Brice mentioned it as well."

For the first time Margaret felt uneasy. "Well, you see, Papa, I . . . I shot him."

"You . . ." Mr. Mayfield put out a shaking hand and found a chair back. Supporting himself upon it, he staggered around to sit down. "I cannot have heard you correctly."

Margaret grimaced. "I'm afraid you did. It is rather complicated. I thought he was chasing me to force me to marry him, so when he came up, I . . . shot him. I had taken your pistol."

"My . . ." He was staring at her as if she had suddenly sprouted horns.

"Yes. I haven't lost it. It's upstairs."

Her father simply continued to stare.

"And so you see that I had to stay and make certain he was all right. I could not leave him bleeding in the road.

The Applebys helped me, and we had the doctor, of course. Oh, and Mrs. Dowling. She is the one who really saved him. I don't know what we should have done without her." Margaret moved a little uncomfortably under her father's astounded gaze.

"And?" he said finally.

"And that is all. Sir Justin is better now, and . . ."

"Exactly. Now what?"

Margaret looked away. "I don't know what you mean."

"I *mean* what is your explanation for the way I found you when I came here tonight? Is that your idea of nursing?"

"N-No." She stopped, at a loss. If he had only delayed his entrance a few minutes, she thought resentfully, she might have been able to tell him what came next. As it was, she wasn't sure.

"If *that* is the sort of goings on . . ."

"It *isn't*. It never happened before."

"I see." Mayfield brightened a little. "Perhaps you are about to tell me that you and Sir Justin are engaged? That the highly unusual circumstances have led to an attachment—"

"No," interrupted Margaret baldly. She could not say that, though she wished she could.

"You were behaving in that scandalous way with a man to whom you are *not* engaged? Margaret, I am deeply shocked." He looked it. "How could you do so? And why?" He shook his head. "You told us you hated the man. What has *happened* to you?"

Margaret looked at the floor. She felt wholly incapable of explaining herself to her father. He would never understand her feelings or her actions. And the one horrid gap in any explanation—the future—loomed large and blank.

"Margaret," repeated Mayfield appealingly. She saw now that he looked tired and sad.

"I . . . I can't talk now," she blurted out. "I will see

you in the morning." And before he could speak again, she ran from the room.

The rest of the inn was quiet. Margaret hurried up the stairs and down the corridor to Keighley's room. If she could just see him for a moment, perhaps all could be settled. But his bedchamber was empty; there was no sign he had been there since dinner. Frustrated, she went to her own room and locked the door. Where could he have gone? And what was he thinking?

The answer to that question would not have pleased Margaret overmuch. Sir Justin was walking along the seawall in the moonlight and thinking that he was a fool. The arrival of Ralph Mayfield had brought back all his former doubts. He remembered how he despised Margaret's family and all their circle, and the anger and repulsion he had felt when her mother had tried to force him into marriage. He recalled his first impression of Margaret herself. She had changed, yes, but could that cowering simpleton really have become the kind of woman with whom he wished to spend his life? Out here, away from her, it seemed impossible. He must have been drunk, to behave as he had tonight, and so must she. It occurred to him now that the chit was probably not accustomed to wine. He did not choose to remember that the small amount he had had could not possibly have addled his wits.

What worried him most was the question of the future. It was obvious what Mayfield would expect and demand, but what of his daughter? Would she come to her senses, as he had, and be horrified at what had passed between them? Once, she had repudiated marriage as vehemently as he. Yet the way she had yielded to his caresses suggested that this attitude might have changed. And if she now took his offer for granted, what would he do? To draw back after tonight was dishonorable, but to be trapped into marriage in such a way—without thought or preparation—galled him. He would not be ruled by the father's threats or the daughter's tears.

By this time Keighley had worked himself into a quite unwarranted state of righteous indignation. With the advent of Mayfield, he suddenly saw not the Margaret he had held this evening but the chit he had angrily come after weeks ago. Unreasonably he blamed everything on her. He *would* not marry such a woman, whatever they might think. He would apologize for his behavior tonight as abjectly as they pleased, but no one else knew of it, so it could not compromise the girl. Her father could take her home again, and everything could be forgotten. And perhaps, after some time had elapsed, he could even see her again . . . He thrust that thought quickly away.

Having decided, Keighley felt better, as if a weight had been lifted from his shoulders. He turned back toward the Red Lion, walking slowly, and rehearsed the calm, measured speech he would use to explain his position to both Mayfields. Perhaps it would not be so difficult as he imagined. Perhaps Margaret would even take his side once the cold light of morning had dissipated the fumes of alcohol.

At the door of the inn he straightened his shoulders, took a breath, and strode in. He hoped everyone was in bed, but such luck could not be counted on. And, indeed, the first thing he saw was Ralph Mayfield's head peering around the door of the back parlor. "Keighley," he exclaimed, "I want to talk to you."

His jaw hardening, Sir Justin joined him. Mayfield shut the door. "Margaret has told me some of what happened," he continued. "It is a very odd story. I should like to hear your version."

"I am sure it is the same as hers."

"Because you have rehearsed her in it?"

Keighley stiffened. "Because there is no need to tell anything but the truth, Mr. Mayfield."

"Ah, the truth."

Their eyes locked in hostility.

"Precisely. Your wife maneuvered me into this ill-starred adventure, and I have carried on as best I could."

The older man looked away. "I have spoken to her about that. I do not at all approve what she did, and she regrets it bitterly, you may be sure."

"As do I." He put a hand to his injured shoulder.

"Did Margaret actually shoot you?"

"She did."

"I wouldn't have thought her capable. But even given that, why did you not send for someone? Me—or one of your own people, at least?"

"I was unconscious for some time. When I recovered, I found that your daughter had spread the story that we were brother and sister, and had been attacked by highwaymen. I could only go along with her unless I wished to start a scandal that was likely to spread far beyond this village. And I was in no state to make other arrangements for a long while, I assure you."

"Hah." Mayfield looked tired. "Well, that is all done with now. I am more interested in what you plan for the future."

"I? Why, to return home now that I am recovered."

"That is all?"

Keighley nodded, bracing himself for what was sure to come.

"And what of Margaret?"

"She will go home with you, I suppose."

"And we simply forget this happened. Is that it?"

"Exactly. Nothing, after all, *has* happened."

"Do you call the scene I walked in on tonight nothing?"

"It was unfortunate, but . . ."

"Un . . ." Mayfield clenched his fists. "Perhaps in the circles you frequent such immorality is merely 'unfortunate.' I, and my friends, do not view it so."

"No doubt."

"Is this to be your attitude? You do not, then, intend to marry my daughter?"

"I do not!"

"You . . . you . . ."

"Never mind, Papa." Unnoticed by the two men in their rage, Margaret had opened the door and was standing just inside it. She wore her blue dressing gown, which molded to her body in soft folds, and her blond hair was hanging in loose waves over her shoulders. She was trembling but this was not evident from across the room. "Sir Justin has made himself very clear. Indeed, I daresay his position is clear to the whole inn. I could hear you both from upstairs. Let us stop broadcasting our affairs, especially since the matter is settled. There is nothing further to say." Her lower lip started to tremble and she pressed her lips together firmly. She wasn't thinking; she was merely reacting, with all the dignity she could muster, to intolerable circumstances. She had obviously made a dreadful mistake with Sir Justin. The thing to do now was to escape as soon as possible. "You look exhausted, Papa," she added. "Come upstairs with me. Mrs. Appleby has prepared her last bedchamber for you."

"Margaret, we *cannot* leave things as they are," responded her father cholerically. He turned to glare at Keighley, whose eyes were fixed on Margaret.

Sir Justin did not notice. He was transfixed by the overwhelming realization that he had made yet another idiotic mistake, and by astonishment at his own newly acquired ineptitude. He had never been so clumsy before. But now, because of his silly meditations and decisions by the shore, he had hurt Margaret terribly. He could see this as if she were transparent. And in doing so, he had finally understood that she was the last person he would wish to hurt. Recent events and conversations had resurfaced, to obliterate his memories of earlier times, and he knew once and for all that he loved her. Ironically, this certainty came just when he had probably lost her forever. Why had he blurted out his stupid refusal for all the inn to hear? Why had he not first discussed the matter with her privately? Common courtesy would have demanded that, after what had passed between them tonight, regardless of his decision.

Keighley ran a hand over his forehead. Mayfield had made him furious, and he had let his temper speak for him, like a fool.

"Father, please," said Margaret. "I really do not want—cannot support—further discussion of this tonight. Let us go to bed."

"But, Margaret . . ."

"He does not *wish* to marry me, Papa," she cried. "And . . . and I do not wish to marry him. So that is that."

"But what about . . ."

"May I just say . . ." began Keighley.

Ralph Mayfield turned on him with burning eyes. "*You*, be quiet, sir. You have no right to say anything, after the way you have behaved."

"I am trying to tell you that . . ."

"Please stop," cried Margaret. "I really cannot bear anymore." She shook her head as if to clear it, her blond curls falling over her face. Sir Justin felt an overwhelming desire to take her in his arms and comfort her. "*I* am going up to bed. I don't wish to see anyone before morning. And you should do the same, both of you." With a sound that might have been a gasp or a sob, Margaret fled.

"See what you have done," accused Mayfield petulantly.

"You were as much at fault," replied Sir Justin, stung.

"I? You, sir, have *ruined* my daughter's life."

"I would say you and your wife did that when you tried to force her to marry in the first place."

"You dare to blame us? I suppose it is our fault that Margaret was kept here, at the mercy of your base desires, that she has become so corrupted as to submit to your embraces and not demand marriage, to be so sullied and degraded—"

"She is no such thing, you old fool."

Ralph Mayfield, pushed beyond endurance by fatigue, emotion, and frustration, stepped quickly forward and landed a highly inexpert punch on Keighley's left cheekbone. Sir Justin, a superb boxer, merely jerked his head with the blow and remained standing. When Mayfield attempted another swipe, Keighley sidestepped. But his rage was boiling up, and he realized that if he remained in the room, he might well indulge in the exquisite pleasure and relief of beating the older man within an inch of his life. As this was clearly out of the question, he backed toward the door, saying, "You are overwrought, Mayfield. Get a grip on yourself. We will talk again in the morning. I have been hasty. Perhaps—"

"*Coward. Poltroon.* Come here where I can reach you." Mayfield swung widely and nearly fell over.

Sir Justin clenched his fists so tightly he felt a twinge in his shoulder, pressed his lips together to stay a blistering retort, and strode out of the room and the inn. Mayfield, left alone, picked up a chair and hurled it against the wall before sinking into another and putting his head in his arms.

Keighley practically ran down the village streets to the sea. He was filled with pent-up emotion—rage at Mayfield and himself, regret, love—and could not stay still. He felt, indeed, as if he would burst unless he found a way to release it. He pounded a fist on the stone seawall, again pulling his nearly healed shoulder, and began to stride along it at a furious pace.

When he came to the curve on the north side of the village, he could see its fleet of boats docked a little farther on, and among them was Jem Appleby's *Gull*. Fixing it with an intent gaze, Keighley began to make his way down to the docks. He would take it out. It was just the sort of foolhardy, physically taxing exploit he wanted to recover his equanimity. It would be hard sailing with one weak arm, and he welcomed the difficulty—exulted in it.

Margaret, who sat at her window watching clouds race across the moon, glimpsed the little boat as it put out into the bay. But she was too miserable even to wonder who could be sailing so late. Tears trickled down her cheeks, to be wiped away with the sleeve of her dressing gown, and she could think of nothing but Keighley's implacable tone when he had said he did not intend to marry her.

16

Margaret did not sleep much that night. She continued to sit in her window and, unknowing, watched a storm blow up over the bay below. First the clouds thickened over the moon as it moved down the sky, finally obscuring it completely, then the wind swooped down and bent the flowering shrubs of the village. At last, just before Margaret retreated to her bed for a few hours, a fitful rain began, blown in sputters against the window glass.

Lying down, she listened. The only sound was the rain; no one moved about the inn. An aching regret filled the last moments before she slept.

She woke early, to an overcast sky and a steady downpour. She rose and dressed and paced about her room for a while, uneasy about going downstairs. Would the morning be a repetition of last night? It was dreadful to hear her father and Sir Justin quarreling so bitterly. The thought of Sir Justin made her shy away again, as she had all night, from examination of her feelings. It was no good thinking; everything had been settled, and there was no more she could do.

In this mood she went down to the parlor and sat at the breakfast table. No one else was about. One of the younger Appleby girls brought tea, and Margaret poured herself a strong cup. What was to be done today? She must face her father, of course. He would urge her to come home with him. Sipping her tea, she shook her head. She could not go back there now; too much had changed. But what would she do?

She had not come to any conclusion when her father came in, still looking tired. She gave him tea, which he drank gratefully, and wondered to herself at how old he looked. She had not noticed before that he was aging.

"Where is Keighley?" he asked when he had finished his tea. He had the air of a man girding for battle.

"I don't know, Papa."

"Still asleep, I suppose. His sort never rises before noon. And a little thing like a girl's ruin would hardly disturb his customary rest."

"Oh, Papa, I wish—"

"Do not say, 'Oh, Papa,' to me, Margaret. I have come to the conclusion that your wits are addled by the trying experiences you have endured. I mean to save you from yourself."

His dismissive tone aroused a spark of anger, which served to lessen Margaret's melancholy. "My wits are better than they ever were," she replied. "And I wish you will not interfere—"

"Interfere? I am your *father*, Margaret. I am responsible for you, and I intend to see you righted."

She raised her eyebrows. "How, Papa?"

"What?"

"How do you plan to do that? I know what you think is right, but Sir Justin has said he will not marry, and I .. . I have agreed. There is nothing you can do."

Her father seemed to swell with rage. "I can have the law on him if necessary."

"I am sure you would not disgrace me in that way."

"Well, I—I—"

"Really, there is nothing more to be done. I think you should go, Papa."

"Go? Home, you mean? I shall not leave this place without you."

Meeting his eyes, Margaret saw that he meant it. How was she to argue with this determination, particularly when she was not certain of her own plans? She did not really want to stay here herself.

She was saved from answering by a tap on the door and the entrance of Mrs. Appleby, who was twisting her apron uncomfortably before her. "Excuse me, miss, but I must speak to you." She cast a sidelong glance at Mr. Mayfield.

"Now, Flos," came Mr. Appleby's voice from the doorway.

"I don't care," responded his wife.

"What is it, Mrs. Appleby?" said Margaret. "Is something wrong?"

"Not to say wrong, miss, but Mr. Camden—The gentleman didn't sleep in his bed last night, and we were wondering if he's left." She looked furtively toward Mayfield again.

Margaret frowned as her father said, "Camden?" in a puzzled tone.

She waved him to silence. "He said nothing to me about leaving, Mrs. Appleby." A cold hand seemed to clutch at her heart as she wondered whether he might have gone without a word.

"His things are still here," put in Mr. Appleby, coming into the room from the corridor. "He hasn't left."

Mrs. Appleby looked unconvinced. "He didn't have much luggage, nothing he couldn't do without."

"His money's locked in the desk drawer," answered her husband disgustedly. "And we shouldn't be bothering folks about him." He, too, looked at Mr. Mayfield, more openly but with more concern.

The latter had realized whom they were speaking of.

"He's gone," Mayfield said positively. "Afraid I'd insist he do the right thing, the blackguard. But he'll have to go back to Devon. We'll find him there."

"Begging your pardon, sir," said Mr. Appleby. "But I don't think he can have gone. His horse is here, too. He'd have no way of traveling without it."

"Probably he is out walking," said Margaret. "He has been doing a great deal of that since he was better."

"And made up his own bed?" asked Mrs. Appleby skeptically.

"Perhaps he didn't sleep. We had a—disagreement last night."

"Yes, miss." Both Applebys looked as though they had heard most of the proceedings.

"I daresay he will return at any moment, wanting his breakfast." Margaret's tone sounded false even to herself.

"Well, I just thought you should know," replied Mrs. Appleby, turning to go. "It's not a question of money, of course. I expect you'll take care of that." With another secret look at Mr. Mayfield, she left them, taking her husband with her.

"He's gone, Margaret," said Mayfield when they were alone again. "He couldn't face the consequences of his dishonorable actions." He sounded somehow satisfied with this idea.

"Will you stop, Papa? Do you care nothing for how I feel?"

He gazed at her in surprise.

Margaret struggled to control her emotions. What if he *had* left her? She realized that she had not entirely given up hope. "I am sure Sir Justin is only out walking."

"Margaret, it is raining. And has been half the night. He would have to be mad to be out in this downpour, and those people thought you so for suggesting it, though they were too polite to say so."

"I . . . I forgot the rain." Looking toward the window,

Margaret saw that it was still coming down heavily.
Something in her gave way, and tears started to trickle
down her cheeks. She could not stop them.

"Here, Margaret," exclaimed her father. "Here, don't
cry. I didn't mean to be so sharp with you. I was angry."
He bustled over and pressed his handkerchief on her.

She took it and dabbed at her eyes, but the tears would
not be dried. The man she loved had fled from her; she
had never felt so alone in her life.

Mayfield hovered anxiously. "What would *you* like to
do, Margaret?" he asked. "Won't you come home with
me and . . . and think things over?"

She couldn't speak, but his tone was so apologetic and
worried that she reached out and squeezed his hand. He
held hers eagerly.

A door slammed nearby, and Margaret looked up. But
it was Jemmy Appleby's voice that sounded in the corridor,
calling for his father, and her head sank down again.

Silence fell in the parlor, broken only by Margaret's
stifled sobs. Her father looked by turns angry and uneasy.
Then, with a second tap on the door, Mr. Appleby
returned, leading Jem by the hand.

"I'm sorry, miss," he said, averting his eyes from
Margaret's tear-stained face. "But Jem here has some
news."

"The *Gull*'s gone," the boy burst out. "I went down
this morning to see to her mooring, and she was *gone*.
And old Ned at the docks says he seen a gentleman take
her out last night."

Margaret sniffed convulsively.

"What is he talking about?" asked her father.

"The *Gull* is his boat," explained Mr. Appleby. "He
and the gentleman and the young lady have been out in
her together."

"He was out in the storm?" gulped Margaret.

"Hard to say, miss—"

"He put out before it started," interrupted Jem. "And he might have gotten to shore several places before it blew up. But where was he going, miss? And why would he take the *Gull* out in the dark? She's a good boat, but she's not fitted for night sailing. Mr. Camden knew that. He knew a deal about boats."

"Enough to get away from here in one, I daresay," replied Mr. Mayfield. "So much for your horses, innkeeper. He has made his escape by water."

Jem appeared to take this suggestion seriously, without considering its implications. "He could have," he agreed. "With sharp sailing, he might have even made Falmouth before the worst of the storm. But you know, miss, with his shoulder the way it was, I wonder if he could handle her properly? The *Gull* takes some quick work when the wind's up."

"I can see no other possible reason for him to have gone out in a boat," answered Mr. Mayfield coldly. "It was hardly the hour for a pleasure cruise."

Mr. Appleby had begun to look doubtful. "It do seem odd," he agreed.

"He would not have been able to sail," cried Margaret. "His shoulder was only just healed, and Mrs. Dowling said he was on no account to strain it. He has had an accident! We must search for him." She looked wildly about, as if half expecting to find Keighley lying broken somewhere nearby.

Mr. Appleby shifted uncomfortably from foot to foot. Mayfield looked thunderous. Only Jemmy appeared to consider her idea possible. "I doubt it, miss," he answered. "What I think is, he probably found the storm too much for him and put in somewhere nearby. Mr. Camden is sharp, and he would have seen that the *Gull* wouldn't hold in that wind, with him not at his best, that is." Jem nodded, with the air of one giving credit where it is due.

"If he hadn't been wounded, I daresay Mr. Camden could have sailed her 'cross the Channel and back again."

Margaret had hung on his words. "What should we do, then?"

Jem shrugged. "The wind's down. I expect he'll bring her back later today." He hunched one shoulder in his father's direction. "I never wanted all this fuss about it."

Mr. Appleby frowned at him, and Mayfield glared at Margaret, but she was too distracted to notice. "We simply wait, then?" she murmured.

"I'll keep watch for him, miss," responded Jemmy, and, pulling free of his father's hand, he went out.

"Margaret," said Mr. Mayfield ponderously.

"I must go out," she said, turning to the door.

"You will do no such thing!"

"Papa, he is out on the water with an injured shoulder, and . . ."

"And what is that to you? This is the man who has destroyed your good character and flatly refused to marry you. The man whom you insisted that *you* did not wish to marry. Why these hysterics?"

"I . . . I can't explain it, Papa. I must—"

"You must do as I say. I command you to pack your things and be ready to go home with me in an hour. I will call for the carriage."

"I *can't*, Papa."

"Are you defying me to my face, Margaret?"

She stared at him. She had never refused any of her parents' demands. Even in running away she had not confronted them. But now it seemed almost easy to reply, "Yes, Papa. I am sorry. I will be back soon."

"*Margaret.*" But she had left the room.

She ran upstairs for her hooded cloak and hurried down again before her father could pursue her with more arguments. Throwing the garment around her, she rushed out into the rain and flung herself down the cobblestones to the seawall. The storm was definitely lessening. Though the rain continued, the wind had calmed to a breeze, and far to the east, lighter sky showed. Margaret bent her head against the raindrops and leaned against the wall, peering out over the water. There was no boat to be seen.

She walked toward the docks, then back around the village to the steps down to the beach. She thought of visiting her pool but rejected the idea, turning to pace back the way she had come. Now that she was alone, her thoughts boiled up and she wondered uneasily whether Sir Justin had indeed used the *Gull* to escape his awkward situation. Why else, indeed, would he go out at such a time?

Shaking her head, she pushed the idea away and looked out to sea again. But though she walked along the seawall most of that day, there was no sign of Keighley or the *Gull*, not even when the clouds broke up at three and the sun illumined the now peaceful waves.

17

It was at this point that Margaret's father insisted she return to the Red Lion. He had come down several times during the day to upbraid her, but now he gave up arguing and simply hauled her along by one arm. Margaret, damp from the rain, cold, and dispirited, did not resist too strongly. Her long, uncomfortable vigil had given her ample time to reconsider, and her conclusions had not been pleasant. Reviewing the events of the past few days, she began to find it easier and easier to believe that Sir Justin had fled to escape her and her father's insistence on marriage. Had he not plainly stated, before them both, that he did not mean to marry her? She had been dazzled by their closeness last night, but now that seemed far away.

And if, as he had said, he was not thinking of marriage, what was she to do? She loved him; that had not changed. But she was still enough her parents' daughter to want the customary setting for that love. Perhaps he, from such a different family, felt differently. Or, and this seemed both more likely and more dreadful to Margaret, perhaps he didn't care for her at all. Perhaps he often kissed girls who, she admitted it, encouraged him to do so, without necessarily feeling anything. His dramatic departure seemed to suggest this was the correct interpretation.

And because she was coming to fear this, she let her father guide her up the hill to the inn and did not protest as he said, "We are leaving at once. I have directed the landlady to pack your things, and I have paid your shot. Keighley's, too, if it comes to that, the blackguard. I imagine he thinks it very amusing that I have been left with his bill. I have the chaise—I have been traveling in it—and James from our stables. He is completely trustworthy and will mention none of this. We can be home tonight, and by tomorrow morning you will have begun to forget this whole terrible incident, Margaret."

The girl wondered confusedly what she should do.

"How it galls me," her father continued in the same ferocious tone, "that we cannot spread the tale of his infamy throughout society. But, of course, that is impossible. I shall drop a word in the ear of one or two of my friends—without giving details, naturally—but for the rest, we must remain silent. It is *unfair*."

"Papa—"

"Now, you needn't say anything, Margaret. I know you are overwrought after all that has befallen you. You can stop worrying now. I will take care of everything."

"But, Papa, you could be wrong. Sir Justin may have had an accident, and if he has, we should—"

"I care nothing for that man. He must take the consequences of his actions. If something has happened to him, well, perhaps it is divine justice, stepping in where we cannot."

This roused Margaret. "You do not *mean* that. Someone must search for him." They had reached the inn by now, and she saw Mr. Appleby and Jem standing before the doorway looking out to sea. Hurrying forward, she said, "Is there to be a search for the *Gull?* I am afraid there may have been an accident."

"Oh, yes, miss," responded Appleby. "Two boats are going out directly, now that the sea's down." He looked skeptical but spoke kindly.

"I'm going," added Jem firmly. "Probably meet him coming back."

Mr. Mayfield made a rude noise.

"What can I do?" asked Margaret.

Both Applebys looked surprised. "Why, nothing, miss," answered the innkeeper after a moment.

"Surely I could be of some help? I could . . ." Margaret could, in fact, think of nothing.

"We'll do everything needful," said Appleby. "Jem here won't spare any pains looking for his boat."

His son assented with heartfelt enthusiasm.

"Yes. Yes, of course," replied Margaret sadly. They were right; there was nothing she could do. And even if there had been, how would Sir Justin respond if she appeared in the search party?

"Is my chaise harnessed up?" interrupted Mayfield. "We will be going soon."

"Yes, sir. She's in the stable, all ready."

"Good. Come, Margaret." He took her arm again.

"We're sorry to see you go, miss," said Mr. Appleby. He eyed her a little anxiously, as if unsure whether to offer help.

"Thank you. You have been very kind to me."

Appleby shrugged, and her father pulled her inside the inn and down the corridor. "Go up and see that they have packed all your things," he said. "And take off that damp cloak. You won't need it. We leave in a quarter hour, Margaret."

At his urging, she walked slowly up the stairs. Her bedchamber, where she had spent so many hours that it now seemed almost like home, was bare and unwelcoming. All her things were folded and lying in a portmanteau she recognized as one of her parents'. Margaret slipped out of her cloak and sat down on the bed. What should she do? If there was any chance that she could help in the search for the *Gull*—but there was not. She could only stand by and wait. She would have done that if she thought Sir Justin would welcome her efforts. But this, too, was doubtful. Yet how could she simply leave with her father, go home again as if nothing had occurred?

With a worried sigh, Margaret stood and went to the window. The sea now sparkled blue under a mostly clear sky. No boat punctuated its bright expanse. She was utterly alone.

Abruptly she thought of Mrs. Dowling. *She* would know what should be done. And she must be paid for her nursing in any case. Snatching up her reticule, Margaret ran back down the stairs and out the door, encountering no one. In five minutes she was knocking on the cottage door and being admitted with a cheerful greeting.

"Mrs. Dowling," she almost gasped.

"Here, now. What's this?"

"Have you heard what has happened?"

"I've heard there's another gentleman at the Red Lion, an *older* gentleman." She cocked an inquiring eye at Margaret. "If the truth be told, I meant to come up there today, but I had to go out to the Woosters' for a birthing."

"It's my father."

"Ah, is it, now?"

"Yes. He's very angry with me."

Mrs. Dowling merely nodded and settled into a listening pose.

"I—I did as you suggested and spoke to—to the other gentleman. But—" She could not continue.

Mrs. Dowling eyed her shrewdly. "You don't mean he denied you?"

"Not exactly." Trembling, Margaret poured out all that had occurred. "So you see," she finished, "he said that he did not want to marry me. And now he is gone. I—I suppose I should just go home with Father, but—"

"But you don't want to."

"No. That is—"

"Of course not." Mrs. Dowling sighed. "Gentlemen *are* foolish. They always make such a muck of things and then expect their ladies to put it right again without so much as a whimper."

"What do you mean?"

"Well, if you'll pardon me, miss, I must say your father went about it exactly wrong."

"About what?"

"And the other gentleman wasn't much better. Cut off his nose to spite his face, he did. Going off in a boat in the dark—just like a little boy sulking. They don't change, miss, from the time they're three and rolling in the dirt cursing one another."

Margaret frowned at her.

"I'll tell you what," the old woman was continuing when they heard shouting in the street outside.

"*Margaret*," bellowed a voice.

"It's Father!"

"*Margaret*." A pounding started on the door, and Mrs. Dowling went to open it. Mr. Mayfield stamped in angrily. "*Here* you are. They said you might have come here. What in heaven's name are you doing, Margaret? The chaise is ready. We are going *now*."

"I . . . I wanted to see Mrs. Dowling. She hasn't been paid for her nursing," added Margaret hurriedly.

"Paid for . . . Dash it, am I supposed to lay out good money for *that* as well? Outrageous. But anything to get away from this cursed place. How much are you owed, woman?"

Margaret protested his mode of address with a gesture, but Mrs. Dowling merely gazed at him. "Not so much as that fancy Falmouth doctor," she replied.

"Rightly so, no doubt. How much?" Mayfield had taken out his purse and was brandishing it impatiently.

"I will pay her, Papa."

"Nonsense."

"She has been very kind to me, and I wanted—"

"Well, thank her and run along, Margaret. We must get on the road at once if we are to benefit at all from the evening light. *Go on.*"

Margaret looked helplessly at Mrs. Dowling, who indicated the door with a small nod. Reluctantly the girl moved toward it. She felt a paralyzing mixture of anger, despair, and fatigue.

"Go on," repeated her father. "Get in the chaise. It is in front of the inn. I shall be there directly."

"Papa."

"*Go*, Margaret."

With a broken sigh, she did so, climbing slowly back toward the inn. She could do no more; everything was spoiled.

In the cottage Mayfield was surveying Mrs. Dowling. "Are you in his pay?" he asked her coldly. "Did you conspire in my daughter's imprisonment?"

The old woman raised her eyebrows.

He made an impatient gesture. "It hardly matters now. How much do you want?" He opened his purse.

"You're botching this job, you know," said Mrs. Dowling.

"I beg your pardon?"

"She'll not be happy without him."

"If you are speaking of my daughter—"

"Nor he without her, if I know anything."

Ralph Mayfield swelled in outrage. Not only had his daughter defied him and her ravisher escaped, but now this old fisherwoman had the temerity to criticize his actions. It was too much. "You don't," he snapped. "You know nothing whatever. Now, if you will be good enough to tell me how much—"

"I know more about them two than you," interrupted Mrs. Dowling. "I've seen it coming. They belong together."

"Can you possibly mean—"

"I mean your daughter and the gentleman. It's plain as the nose on your face."

"No doubt that is why Kei—the 'gentleman' has taken to his heels and left my daughter here."

"Oh, that was because of you. If you hadn't come, all would have been well."

Mayfield had to take a breath before he could speak. "You *were* in his pay. So I spoiled your little game, eh? Both of you. If I had not come, Margaret would have been seduced—I caught him at that—and kept here as long as she interested him, I suppose. You—you— It sickens me to think of it."

Mrs. Dowling shook her head. "You are a thick one, aren't you?"

"How much?" answered Mayfield through clenched teeth.

She named a small sum, and he threw it down on the table. "You'd do better to—"

"*Enough,*" he roared. "If I find that you have been near my daughter again, I shall have the law on you." And he slammed out of the cottage.

"Highty-tighty," said Mrs. Dowling. She put two fingers to her lips, then hurried out her back door and along certain narrow passages up to the Red Lion.

Owing to her superior knowledge of the village, she reached the inn before Mr. Mayfield. Seeing the chaise pulled up before the front door, she looked inside, but the vehicle was empty. She slipped through the inn door and looked in the parlor. Here she found Margaret slumped in a chair, one hand over her eyes. "Miss," she hissed, causing the girl to start. "Here, leave your direction with the Applebys. I'll send for you if he comes back." And before Margaret could reply, she was gone again.

In the next moment Margaret heard her father calling her. But she ran to the writing desk and wrote out her real name and address on a scrap of notepaper. After a moment's hesitation she also scribbled a short note to Sir Justin and sealed it. She was just finishing when her father strode in and demanded, "Why aren't you in the chaise?"

"Coming, Father." She rose, putting the hand that held the letters behind her.

He gestured impatiently, and she followed him into the corridor.

"I will just say good-bye to Mrs. Appleby."

"You have done that."

"She was so kind." Not waiting for an argument, Margaret darted toward the kitchen. Mrs. Appleby and her daughters were there, and she mumbled a good-bye as she thrust the papers into the woman's hands. Before her father could protest further, she was back and heading toward the front door. "All right, Papa," she said.

Mayfield watched her back speculatively, then he frowned and walked to the kitchen. Mrs. Appleby was still standing as Margaret had left her, looking perplexedly at the letters in her hand.

"I'll just take those," said Mayfield, taking them from her and substituting a gold sovereign. "We are on our way. Good day, Mrs. Appleby."

"But the young lady . . ."

"Good day." He turned on his heel and left her staring, joining Margaret in the chaise before she realized that he had delayed.

Margaret did not afterward remember much of the ride home. They hardly spoke, and she was sunk in her own despondent thoughts. She could not keep herself from recalling her days with Keighley, the picnic, their talks—their embrace. That last evening came back to her again and again. It was like a happy dream that had turned to a nightmare. She would remember how he had held her and looked at her, and then it would all dissolve with a crash and the sound of her father's voice.

What was she going to do? she wondered over and over. Her home in Devon now seemed a prison to which she was being inexorably dragged. She might never speak to Keighley again. What would she do?

18

When Sir Justin had cast off the lines, pushed out from the dock, and raised the *Gull*'s small sail, he immediately felt better. There was a good breeze, and the little boat at once began to skim along the water away from the village. He took great lungfuls of rushing air and, with one hand on the tiller and the other holding the mainsheet, felt himself start to relax.

The waves were choppy but small, and the moon shed a fitful light over them. The movement of the *Gull* was both exhilarating and soothing. Keighley tacked back and forth across the bay, heading generally toward its mouth and the open sea, though he did not intend to enter it. He felt at one with the vessel, leaning as she leaned and breasting each wave with her, wholly in control, a feeling he particularly relished after this evening. The sensations were so pleasant that he paid no attention to the weather, as he certainly would have at any other time, and thus did not notice the gradual thickening of the clouds and the stepping up of the wind. Only when a few drops of rain spattered his face did he gaze upward, and then he frowned and cursed and turned the little boat back toward its berth.

By this time, however, it was too late. The squall had

blown up over the bay, and the waves were cresting higher with each moment. As he tried to hold the *Gull* on course for the village an especially violent gust of wind hit her, making the sail crack and wrenching the controlling rope from his hand. In an instant all was chaos. The sail flapped wildly; the boat wallowed in the wave trough and rocked so deeply that it shipped water on each side in turn. And Keighley lay back in the stern, his teeth clenched in pain, gripping his injured shoulder with a desperate hand. The unexpected pull had strained it beyond bearing, and it now felt as it had not for weeks. He could scarcely move the arm, let alone pull in the sheet again.

The boat rocked madly, adding to the disorienting effect of the pain. Keighley felt dizzy and confused. But finally he crouched and carefully reached for the rope with his good arm. Holding it loosely, he slid back by the tiller, sitting in the bottom of the *Gull* and draping his wounded shoulder over it, the arm curled around its length. Gingerly he pulled in the rope until the sail tightened slightly and caught the wind. He could hardly hold it, even luffing slightly. However, with the wind once again pushing the boat, he could at least steer a bit, and he looked around to find the closest refuge, all thoughts of the village gone.

From his low position he could see no land. He considered trying to stand but rejected the idea as too dangerous in his present condition. The easiest choice was simply to run before the wind. It was coming from the sea and thus must drive him to shore eventually. Whether he could last so long, or the boat stay afloat in these waves, he did not know, but there was no other choice.

Keighley thrust himself against the tiller, almost crying out at the pain this caused in his shoulder, and turned the craft in the proper direction. The sail swung out perpendicular to the small mast, and he managed to tie the rope to the cleat provided, though clumsily. Now he need only keep the tiller straight and the boat would find land. He draped himself over it and prayed that it would not be too long before it did so.

For what seemed hours he crouched there, the pain growing worse. But he hung onto the tiller grimly, keeping it steady when the waves tried to knock it aside. Once, when the *Gull* crested a particularly large swell, he thought he saw land ahead and his hopes soared. But in the next moment a sudden gust of wind hit the taut sail, the boat groaned with the impact, and the mast snapped in two at the base.

The craft nearly capsized there and then, all but ending Keighley's adventure. The sail and mast fell over the side and, dragging in the water, pulled the hull over with them. All forward motion ceased, and the boat again began to pitch and roll drunkenly in the waves. Panting, Sir Justin crawled slowly forward, thinking with each heave of the deck that he would lose his hold and fall into the water. But he reached the base of the mast without accident and there found, to his profound relief, that it was broken through. He would not have to try to cut it free in this confusion; he need only heave it and the sail overboard.

This, however, was easier thought than done. Keighley found it abominably difficult to lift the heavy mast and sodden sail while maintaining a secure position in the pitching boat. He would get the shaft raised six inches and start to push it from the craft only to lose his balance and be forced to drop it in order to grab something and steady himself. This occurred over and over, and his shoulder was becoming almost unbearably painful before he at last managed, with the aid of a surge of water, to be rid of the sail. It floated away behind like a fallen cloud.

The *Gull* at once rode higher. But it had taken a good deal of water, which sloshed back and forth with each roll, and there was now little hope of steering. Keighley put his head on his arms on the front decking and tried to summon the energy to crawl back to the tiller. He should at least try. But, incredibly, he felt sleep pulling him. Simply to drop off in this rocking vessel seemed infinitely desirable, to forget everything and let fate take him where it would.

Raising his head, he shook it sharply. The pain was exhausting and confusing him, but he could not give up. He inched back toward the stern, groaning aloud once when the waves slammed the decking into his supporting hand and arm, and at last regained his former position draped over the tiller. He could try to keep the craft headed into the wind and not let her be swamped by the waves; there was nothing else to be done.

Another time passed, again seeming endless to Keighley, though it was only an hour. The *Gull* shipped more water and began to roll like an overfed pig. His head dropped onto his chest, and he drifted between consciousness and oblivion, a red stain starting to spread over his wounded shoulder. And then, without warning, the bottom grated on rock.

Keighley jerked upright. The night had thickened, but he could see a darker mass looming above him. He had reached land. The *Gull* again heaved forward, scraping on the sand, and in one final, desperate effort, he lunged forward, scrambling over the bow and into the water. It came only to his knees, and he somehow dragged the boat farther up until it seemed secure on a narrow beach. Then, completely drained, he pitched to the ground beside it and knew no more.

He woke to heavy rain. Though he could not tell how much time had passed, he was soaked through and shivering. He started to lever himself up and fell back with a cry when he put weight on his injured shoulder. It burned more fiercely than it had since the shooting. But the pelting rain made him try again. He must find shelter. He staggered to his feet and looked about. Perhaps there was a house. Shadows, shot through with spots of light, seemed to dance before his eyes. He thought he saw something, then realized that there was nothing there. Fever, he thought fuzzily. He moved inland but almost at once struck a steep rise that defeated his exhausted energies, and he returned to the sand. There he nearly tripped over the *Gull*, which was lying overturned just above the wave line. He fell to his knees beside it. If he could get under, he would be dry.

The front of the boat had fallen on a small hillock, leaving a narrow opening through which a man might just squeeze after scooping out a bit of sand. With agonizing slowness, Keighley did this, and after a while was able to crawl beneath the hull and lie flat. It felt good to be out of the now driving rain, and he relaxed without another thought into unconsciousness once again.

He did not rouse until the returning sun made the boat an oven of damp heat, and even then he only writhed from side to side and called out broken words, his body drenched with sweat. It was thus that Jem Appleby found him the following morning, when he and two helpers raised the *Gull* and turned it over. Keighley did not recognize them or indeed seem to realize that he had been rescued. His breath came in great rasps, and his skin was mottled red.

"Lor'," commented Jem. "He do look bad. We'd best get him home as soon as may be."

"How do you suppose he came to the island?" wondered one of the others, a weather-beaten sailor of fifty.

"He knew it," answered Jem. "I brought him here. Perhaps he made for it when he saw the storm coming up." He looked at the *Gull* with a mixture of doubt and deep sorrow. "Or perhaps he was blown here. Looks like it. Come on. Help me carry him to the boat."

"Shall we take the *Gull?*" asked the other, slipping his hands under Keighley's legs and heaving him up.

"We'll see if she'll tow. I don't want to leave her here."

In this way they returned to the village, Keighley lying oblivious across the gunwales and the *Gull* wallowing disconsolately along behind. Their arrival attracted some attention, and a small crowd gathered to watch them carry Sir Justin along the dock and up toward the Red Lion.

"Someone run ahead and tell my mother," panted Jem. "And fetch Mrs. Dowling. The gentleman's took bad."

Two onlookers ran to do these errands, and by the time the little procession reached the inn both Mrs. Appleby and Mrs. Dowling were outside waiting for them. They carried Keighley upstairs to his bedchamber, and the latter examined him. "Fever," she pronounced positively. "And he's opened his wound again. He's bad."

Mrs. Appleby wrung her hands. "What shall we do?"

"Nurse him, of course. I'd best move in here for a few days, Floss. Annie can help me. He'll need watching for a while."

"Yes. Yes, of course. But—I mean, after everything that has happened—"

Mrs. Dowling shrugged. "This gentleman will die if we don't take care. That's all I know just now. Will you find me some hot water, Floss? And ask Dan to come up and help me lift him."

The other wrung her hands again. "Dan's gone into Falmouth for supplies."

"Then you'll have to help me yourself. Or Jem. Get Jem. And that hot water. Quickly, now."

With a small moan, Mrs. Appleby hurried out. The next half hour was a flurry of bathing, bandages, and cold compresses, but at the end Mrs. Dowling pronounced herself more satisfied. "He's very hot," she told the others. "It's a pity it's not cooler out. But he may do. I'll sit with him. You can go. Send Annie at dinnertime."

The Applebys left her. Mrs. Dowling took some knitting out of the bag she had brought with her and sat down in the armchair near the bed. With only occasional interruptions to change the compress on Keighley's forehead, she knitted through the afternoon, her blue worsted square growing steadily larger.

At four Sir Justin seemed to worsen. He thrashed about in the bed as if the covers chafed him and rolled his head from side to side. Mrs. Dowling tried to soothe him with a fresh compress, but he shook it off and abruptly muttered, "Margaret. *Margaret.*"

"There, now," responded his nurse. "You lie back. It's no good calling her now."

"Must get back," he said more loudly. He made as if to throw back the covers. "Must speak."

Mrs. Dowling pushed firmly down on his good shoulder. "Not now, you mustn't. You need to rest first. It will wait."

"Margaret," he murmured again. "Didn't mean it."

Clucking soothingly and thrusting him gently down, Mrs. Dowling managed to calm him. But these episodes recurred twice during the afternoon, and just before Annie was to relieve her for dinner, Keighley sat bolt upright and positively shouted, "*Margaret.* You must listen to me. I didn't mean it." When his nurse clasped his forearms, he looked at her without recognition and repeated himself.

"Yes, indeed, sir. She'll listen. I guarantee you that."

Some spark of consciousness seemed to appear in Sir Justin's face. "I made a mistake," he told Mrs. Dowling earnestly. "A terrible mistake."

"Well, we all go wrong now and then. You'll make it right when you're better."

"She doesn't know. She thinks I meant it. I must tell her at once."

"You will tell her, but not until you rest summat. Now lie back." Her practiced commanding tone reached him, and he obeyed, but he remained restless.

When Annie came in, he sat up again. "*You* tell her," he exclaimed, still hovering between lucidity and delirium.

"All right, all right, sir. I'll do my best," agreed the old woman. "You behave youself now for Annie, and I'll be back in a bit."

"Tell her," he insisted.

"I'll send word at once."

This seemed to satisfy Keighley for the moment, and Mrs. Dowling went downstairs to find Mrs. Appleby. "We must send for the young lady," she told her. "He insists on speaking to her, and I believe it will do him good."

The landlady nodded. "I thought there was something there."

"*You* thought they were brother and sister," snorted Mrs. Dowling derisively.

"Well, they said so."

"*Said.* But that's by the by. We must send a letter. You or Dan will have to write. I'm no hand at it."

Mrs. Appleby nodded again. "Jem can carry it. He's been moping about like a sick cat."

"What's her direction? Is it far?"

"What do you mean? I don't know it. I thought you did."

"I? She was to leave her name and direction with you. I told her to."

"Well, she didn't."

"She said she would."

"I can't help that. She . . . Wait a minute."

Mrs. Dowling scowled impatiently. "We haven't a deal of minutes *to* wait."

"That must have been the paper she gave me."

"It must, indeed. Go and fetch it, Floss, you silly woman."

The other drew herself up. "I can't do that. The gentleman took it away again. The one who *said* he was her father."

"What? Why did you let him do a thing like that?"

"I didn't know what it was. Nobody tells *me* anything."

"What happened, exactly?"

"The young lady came into the kitchen, where we were at the baking. She said they were going, and she pushed some papers into my hand and ran out again. The next moment, the gentleman was there, taking the papers and giving me a coin. I never knew what they were." She met Mrs. Dowling's disgusted look squarely.

"Of all the—What are we to do, then?"

"I'm sure I don't know."

"We must find the girl."

"She said her name was Camden."

"And so, of course, it is not. Did she never mention where she lived?"

"Not to me. You can ask Dan and the others."

"I shall. But what an underhanded trick." She scowled again. "That father has a deal to answer for."

"Do you think he *was* her father?" asked Mrs. Appleby avidly.

"Oh, yes. No question about that. But how are we to find her? I must speak to Jem. Where is he?"

"He's supposed to be in the stables. But I imagine he's down at the dock mooning over his boat.

"Send someone—No, I'll go down myself."

"Why do you need the young lady so badly?" wondered Mrs. Appleby. "They quarreled more than they got on."

Mrs. Dowling gazed at her with contempt, shook her head, and went out without answering. The landlady looked after her angrily for a moment, then shrugged and went back to the kitchen.

Everyone who had spoken to Margaret or Keighley was questioned closely, but no one could remember anything about their homes. It might have been mentioned, admitted several, but if so it had gone right out of their heads again. By the end of that day Mrs. Dowling was seething with exasperation and so snappish that everyone avoided her when possible, not liking to be called dolts to their faces.

Only when she again took her place beside Keighley's bed did the old woman's face soften. "It's a muddle we're in, and no mistake," she told him softly. He breathed raspingly on, unknowing. "If the young lady knew, she'd be here in an instant. But how to tell her? She'll think you weren't found or that you don't care to see her. Tch, tch." She took her seat again and set her jaw. "Not if I can help it," she muttered. "Not if I have anything to say."

Sir Justin's fever did not abate the following day. Rather, it increased until by nightfall he was burning in a raving delirium, no longer making any sense and in real danger. The combination of his half-healed wound, overexertion in the storm, and the night and day of exposure had pushed him to the brink of death. Mrs. Dowling did not leave his bedside. She changed compresses, poured cooling drinks down his throat, and wished for something more to do. As always in such cases, she complained that there was not some drug that would lower a fever.

On the morning of the third day he was much the same after a difficult night. Mrs. Dowling, who had been looking older as the hours passed and now seemed even more like Margaret's picture of a witch, sought out Jem Appleby in the cool dawn and said, "You must go and ask along the road for the young lady."

"I don't know which way they went," he protested.

"Ask."

"But—"

"Don't argue with me, boy. Do you want the gentleman to die?"

"*No.*"

"Well, then, we must find the young lady, wherever she's gone. He calls for her night and day, and I can't make him rest."

"I don't even know her name. And, besides, no one will tell *me.*"

"Are you trying to claim you can't do it?" Mrs. Dowling glared at him, her eyes red rimmed from hours of watching.

Jem hung his head. "P'raps I can, but—"

"Well, then *go.*"

"Will it really help the gentleman?" The boy looked torn. He had been spending every free hour repairing the *Gull.*

"Nothing else will help as much, I promise you."

"All right. I'll try. But I don't say I can find her."

"Trying's all I ask. You're a good lad, Jem."

He squirmed. "Don't know what Mum will say."

"I'll see to her, and Dan as well. You get ready."

"Need some money."

She nodded and waved him away. As Jem went out the back door to the stables Mrs. Dowling started slowly up the stairs, muttering inaudibly to herself.

19

Margaret's reunion with her mother was strained. Mrs. Mayfield heard the chaise pull up before the house late in the evening, and she was out on the front steps by the time they had climbed out. She bore down on Margaret like a ship in full sail, folded her in her arms for a brief instant, then held her away and said, "*Where* have you been?" in a tone that belied her first affectionate gesture.

Margaret merely slipped out of her grasp and went inside. Mrs. Mayfield looked startled and opened her mouth to speak, but her husband waved her into the library, leaving their daughter to do as she pleased.

She went upstairs. Her old bedroom seemed strange and alien when she walked in, like a place she had inhabited long ago and almost forgotten. She touched the bedpost and the dressing table, opened the wardrobe and gazed at the row of dresses there—she would be able to wear something other than the three gowns she had had in Cornwall. It all seemed unreal. It is as if, Margaret thought, I were only half here. I see and feel things as if through gauze. Her mind was still full of the village, the ocean, and, perpetually, Justin Keighley. Had he returned to the inn? she wondered. What would he tell the Applebys?

She heard footsteps on the stairs. Her mother was coming up. Unhesitatingly Margaret did something she had never done before in her life. She stepped forward and turned the key in her bedroom door, locking it securely. She had had enough for today.

The doorknob rattled, then there was a sharp knock on the panels. Margaret stood still and silent. She expected her mother to call out, but she did not. Instead, after rattling the knob once more, she walked away. When her footsteps died out, Margaret breathed a sigh and started to undress. She didn't think she would sleep, but there was nothing else she could do just now.

In the morning she delayed going downstairs as long as possible. She had indeed slept poorly, dreaming of storms and waking to lie rigid in her bed, and she did not look forward to this day. But at last she could put it off no longer. She walked down to the breakfast room through empty corridors and found her mother there, her place cleared, writing a letter.

Margaret stopped briefly in the doorway, then slipped into her place and poured out a cup of tea. Her mother continued to write without looking up.

The girl took a muffin from under a silver cover and began to butter it. Her mother paid no attention.

Margaret glanced sidelong at her as she raised the muffin to her lips. Mrs. Mayfield's jaw was set, but this was by no means unusual. Could it be that she was to escape a lecture? She bit into the muffin, and her mother said, "So?" in a penetrating tone.

Margaret choked a little, chewed and swallowed.

"What have you to say for yourself?"

"Nothing, Mama," replied the girl wearily.

"Nothing. Well, I suppose there is very little you *can* say, but I would have expected some attempt at excusing your reprehensible behavior."

Margaret kept her eyes on her plate and sipped her tea.

"Well?"

"I am not going to argue with you, Mama. I tried with Father, and it does no good."

Mrs. Mayfield looked both surprised and frustrated. "What do you mean, it does no good?"

"You will not see my side."

"I should think *not*. Could you really expect me to condone your refusing to marry a man who has utterly compromised you? When your father told me what he found in Cornwall, I could scarcely believe my ears. Actually in that libertine's arms, and then both of you saying you *would* not marry. Could you imagine I would accept such a thing?"

"No, Mama." Margaret's voice, in contrast to her mother's, remained quiet and unemotional. She felt as if she had used up all her store of feelings; there were none left to throw into argument.

Mrs. Mayfield stared at her. "What has happened to you, Margaret?" She surveyed her more closely. "Your looks are improved, I must admit—greatly improved. But I cannot say the same for your character. Indeed, I can hardly believe you are my daughter."

The girl shrugged slightly and took another bite of muffin. Her mother glared at her, started to speak, then paused and reconsidered. After a while she continued in a different tone. "What do you intend to do, then?"

Margaret looked up, meeting her eyes.

"You refuse to talk to me," said Mrs. Mayfield. "What *will* you do?"

"I—I had thought of working."

"What?"

"I—I should like to help people, Mama. I thought of going to London and finding work on one of the relief committees. The poor are—"

"You? Work in the slums of London? Have you gone mad, Margaret?"

Her daughter turned her head away.

"I have never heard such idiocy in my life. It is out of the question. You have no idea what you would find."

"I have some idea."

"Nonsense. I believe you are a bit mad. The terrible experiences of the last weeks have turned your brain." Mrs. Mayfield seemed pleased with this notion. She appeared to turn it over in her mind.

Margaret was finally getting angry. "What do you suggest I do, then?" she asked. "According to you, I am ruined. Do you wish me simply to pine away out of remorse?"

"On the contrary," her mother responded eagerly. "I think if we put a bold face on this thing, we can pass it off without much more gossip. There *was* talk, of course, when you disappeared. Particularly since Sir Justin left at the same time. But we put it about that you had gone to stay with your aunt, and now we can simply say that you are returned from your visit. After the first whispers the matter will die down and be forgotten, I daresay."

Margaret shrugged.

"There is a luncheon at the Camdens on . . ."

At the mention of this name Margaret stiffened. "I couldn't possibly be less interested in what our neighbors say of me," she snapped.

Mrs. Mayfield drew herself up. "You cannot mean that."

"I assure you I do."

Her mother stared at her incredulously. Her angry expression wavered. "And do you care nothing for *me?* Because *I* am very conscious of our position both here and in town. And what of your father's career? Are you trying to ruin him as well as yourself?"

Margaret met her intent blue gaze. Abruptly she realized that the flicker visible in the back of her mother's eyes was a kind of terror, and her opposition melted. She really did not care what people like the Camdens said, and since she did not, it was all one to her whether she saw them or not. "You want me to go to this luncheon?" she asked.

Mrs. Mayfield leaned forward. "Yes. And we will tell them—"

"That I have been visiting my aunt. You may tell them what you like, Mama. I shall not contradict you. When is this party?"

"Next Monday."

Margaret could hardly bear the intense eagerness in her mother's gaze. "Very well. I shall do whatever you like about it."

Her mother did not actually thank her, but the heartfelt sigh she gave as she leaned back in her chair demonstrated her gratitude and the depth of the concern she had been feeling.

"But here at home I will not be badgered," added Margaret, extracting some exchange for her concession.

Mrs. Mayfield eyed her, some of her old truculence returning to her face. "I do not see—"

"Because if you and Papa are continually lecturing me, I shall simply run away again." Margaret rose and stared down at her.

Her mother frowned and pressed her lips tightly together, far from defeated. But her silence was enough for Margaret, and she turned and left the room.

Her satisfaction at this victory was short-lived, however. Before she had regained her bedchamber, she was again thinking of Justin Keighley and of their ill-fated moments together. Where was he? Why had he run away without a word to her? And why had she let herself be dragged home before finding out what had become of him?

This last question almost sent her to the stables for her horse. But then she recalled the Applebys' discouragements and, more important, Keighley's rejection. She had been right to leave. The Applebys or Mrs. Dowling would write her if there was any news.

The next two days were agonizing. Margaret could not settle to any pursuit. She tired to read, walk, sew, but each time she found herself gazing blankly into space after the first few minutes, lost to the present. Her parents treated her warily, as one might a strange wild animal, and generally left her alone. When they met at meals, Margaret scarcely spoke, and the Mayfields exchanged worried glances. They were particularly concerned when, on the third day, she ordered her horse. But this time Margaret noticed their looks and said, "You needn't worry. I am only going for a ride in the neighborhood."

She did not take a groom, in defiance of her mother's rule, and once she was out galloping across the fields, she felt somewhat better. She had not ridden like this in the past. Then she had trotted sedately along the lanes, her servant just behind. But now she felt she wanted to hurl herself over hedges, splash through streams, throwing up water on every side, and race the mail coach down the high road. Somehow, she thought, a great spring of energy had been released in her, and it would never be stopped again.

She had turned back toward home when suddenly she got an idea. She was not too far from Keighley's house; she could easily swing past it on her way.

Even if Keighley did not mean to communicate with her, he must send word to his servants. She might be able to find out something there. He might even have returned home.

Her heart began to pound as she pulled her horse's

head around and headed toward his house. If he *were* there, what would he say to her? She quickly reached the wall surrounding his park and rode to the front gate. The grounds looked deserted. For a moment she wavered. It was unusual, unheard of, really, for an unchaperoned young lady to visit a single gentleman. The servants would be shocked. But then she grimaced and started up the drive. Her purpose overrode convention.

At the house she slid off her horse and strode up to knock before she could lose her nerve. The door was opened by a footman. "Hello," said Margaret. "I wish to inquire whether Sir Justin has yet returned from his . . . his journey?"

The footman, who had seemed surprised to find her alone on the doorstep, shook his head. "No, miss. He's still away."

"Did he say when he would be back?" asked Margaret valiantly.

"Not so far as I know, miss."

"I—I see." She wondered if she dared go further, then decided she had nothing more to lose. "Could you inquire? I wished to speak with him about a rather important business matter."

"Yes, miss. If you'll step in?" The man seemed only too glad to refer this problem to a superior.

"I must stay with my horse."

He looked uneasy but disappeared into the rear of the hall. In a few moments he returned, accompanied by a stately butler. "May I be of some assistance?" inquired the latter.

Margaret repeated her request.

"I'm sorry, miss, but Sir Justin has given no indication when he plans to return," answered the butler. "Perhaps you should write. I'll see that he gets the letter as soon as he arrives."

"Or perhaps I could send it wherever he is staying," responded Margaret, amazed at her own effrontery.

The butler looked slightly uncomfortable. "Unfortunately I am not at liberty to give out his address."

It was clear to the girl that he did not know it. "Oh? Well, then, I suppose I must do as you suggest. Thank you."

"Certainly, miss."

She remounted at the mounting block and trotted back down the drive, frowning meditatively. At least she had made sure there was no news from Keighley. She was glad to know that, but it left her as perplexed as ever over what had happened to him.

The week passed in this fashion, and Monday arrived all too soon. Having promised to attend the Camdens' entertainment, Margaret felt she must, but she did not look forward to the afternoon. As she put on a white muslin gown sprigged with pink flowers and her straw hat, she watched her reflection with astonishment. It appeared so familiar, so unconcerned. How could her mind and body be so at odds?

Mrs. Camden had arranged tables on the lawn for luncheon, and most of the other guests had arrived when the Mayfields walked out to them. Margaret saw the Twitchels, and was immediately reminded of that long-ago dinner party at which everything had begun. Her own presence seemed to be attracting a good deal of attention.

The Camdens came to greet them, and Mrs. Mayfield told her story. Margaret was just back from a long visit to her aunt. She had had a splendid time. And wasn't she looking well? Mrs. and Mrs. Camden agreed, though they kept casting sidelong glances at her, as if not quite sure whether to speak directly to her. "Come and say hello," said their hostess finally, when Mrs. Mayfield had run down. "You know everyone, I think."

At first Margaret's mother kept close at her side, and there was little discussion of her absence. But when luncheon was served, they were seated at separate tables, and Margaret saw, with a sinking sensation, that Maria Twitchel and Alice Camden were both members of her party. Between the former's acid inquisitiveness and the latter's naive wonder, she was probably in for an unpleasant time.

Predictably Mrs. Twitchel leaned forward as soon as they were seated and said, "I understand you had a delightful stay with your aunt, Margaret."

Margaret nodded unencouragingly.

"Such a distinguished woman, I thought when we met last year. How are her two dear boys?"

But Margaret was not so easily caught. "Hardly boys now, Mrs. Twitchel. Ronald is up at Oxford, and Dennis just finished his last year at Eton. They were not home this summer. Reading parties."

"Really. How interesting."

"Do you know that Sir Justin Keighley has been away also?" offered Alice Camden, seemingly unaware of the delicacy of this subject. Eyeing her, Margaret wondered if anyone could be so truly innocent and decided they could not.

"Yes," agreed Maria Twitchel eagerly. "Is it not strange? We have not seen *either* of you since your parents' dinner party in July. It seems so long ago now. And no one seems to know where Sir Justin has gone." Her eyes bored into Margaret's. "I don't suppose *you've* heard, Margaret?"

"I? Why should *I* hear?"

Mrs. Twitchel shrugged. "Oh, one does, sometimes."

"I haven't the least idea where he may be," replied Margaret truthfully. Her tone seemed to both convince and disappoint her hearers.

"I was so sorry to read about your engagement," said Alice Camden then. "Mr. Manningham seemed such a *nice* young man."

Margaret knew that her parents had sent a notice to the *Morning Post* announcing the end of her engagement. "Wasn't he?" she agreed cordially. She was rather enjoying this exchange, something she would never have predicted. "You must look for him when you go to London next season."

Alice blushed and fell silent.

"Do you plan to go as well?" inquired Mrs. Twitchel, by no means daunted by the new, assertive Margaret. "A *second* season is always pleasant. One knows just what to do."

Margaret shrugged.

"Oh, you must insist. I daresay your mother will be only too glad to have you with them once again." They all looked over at Mrs. Mayfield, who unluckily was at this moment glancing toward her daughter. Everyone smiled nervously and looked away again.

"Peaches," exclaimed Margaret in an effort to change the subject as dessert was brought out. "How lovely they are. I haven't had fresh peaches all summer."

"I thought your aunt had trees."

Margaret swallowed. Her aunt *did*; she was immensely proud of her fruit. "They got the blight," she answered, callously sacrificing her aunt's orchard and praying she would not tomorrow send them a bushel of its produce.

"A pity," said Mrs. Twitchel.

The rest of the meal passed relatively calmly, and the gentlemen at the table were allowed to make a few innocuous remarks about the fine weather. Margaret escaped as soon as possible and joined the guests who were beginning to congregate on the terrace, under the awning. Her father was there, and she went to stand at the edge of his group.

"It's ridiculous," Mr. Twitchel was saying to him. "All they can talk of is reform, reform. They cannot seem to understand that giving in to these disgraceful tactics—riots, machinery breaking, arson—will only encourage the riffraff who instigate them. And then we shall see chaos. Give that sort of man the vote? *Preposterous*."

Mr. Mayfield was nodding sagely when he suddenly froze at the sound of his daughter's voice saying, "Perhaps if they had the vote, they would not feel obliged to express their wishes in such violent ways."

The men in the group turned to stare at her. Mr. Twitchel's mouth fell open, and he looked as astonished as if Mrs. Camden's pug dog had spoken. "*Margaret*," said Mr. Mayfield.

"Surely, Father, you can see how maddening it must be to have no voice in government when the laws passed are grinding your life away? Now, if the laborers had the vote, they would feel—"

"*Laborers*," sputtered Mr. Twitchel. "You must be joking."

"Margaret knows nothing whatever about—"

"Yes, I do, Papa. I have done some reading and visited a number of poor families." Margaret had become engrossed in the discussion, and the desire to show her new knowledge made her forget the need for concealment. "I saw firsthand how badly off they are. Really, something must be done for them."

"Margaret," said Mayfield more weakly. He looked like a boxer who has taken a telling blow.

"If one tries to help them, they merely stop working and come to expect charity," said Twitchel.

"I can't believe that is true. Every man I spoke to wanted desperately to work. Often they could not find employment."

"There is work for anyone who wants it," countered

Mr. Twitchel smugly. "They must learn to accept the jobs there are, rather than reject them as low or degrading."

"But, Mr. Twitchel, I assure you that there *were* no jobs. They did not want . . ."

Their voices had risen, and most of the guests had turned to see what was happening. Margaret's mother was even now bearing down on the group with a set expression. Abruptly Margaret recalled where she was and to whom she spoke. This was not like talking to Sir Justin, who had been interested in her opinions. Here she was merely a silly young girl, and even had she been respected, she would never convince the likes of John Twitchel, or her parents.

"Margaret," said her mother in a commanding tone, "I think it is time we were going. You are still overtired from your journey."

With a slight shrug, Margaret agreed. Her mother, gathering her stunned husband, said their good-byes, and herded them to the carriage in front of the house. Not until they were inside and driving home did she add, "What has come over you, Margaret? I have never been so mortified."

Margaret smiled sadly. "I appear to have become a radical."

Her father gasped, but her mother said, "*Nonsense.* These ridiculous ideas will disappear in time, and you will wonder how you came to be so foolish." But she did not sound entirely convinced by her own words, and an uneasy silence fell in the vehicle.

Margaret gazed out the window. Everything was dreadful. Baiting the neighbors had been slightly amusing, but she did not care if she never saw any of them again. She wanted only one thing, and that she could not have.

As she thought this she suddenly saw something that made her stiffen and cry, "*Stop.* Stop the carriage." The.

driver, hearing her, pulled up so abruptly that her mother was thrown into her father's arms, and Margaret hurled herself out into the road. "Jem," she cried. "Jem Appleby." And the boy who had been wearily riding toward them on a large cob raised his head, grinned, and waved.

20

The Mayfields' greeting of Jem was by no means as enthusiastic as their daughter's. They refused to allow him in the coach, insisted, in fact, that Margaret rejoin them at once and come home. Seeing her mother's irate expression, the girl complied. She did not want to talk to Jem in their presence in any case. But as soon as they reached the house she was out and holding the boy's mount so that he could slide off. "What has happened?" she asked him in a low voice. "Why did your father not write me?"

Jem leaned against his horse's side, looking tired.

"Margaret," snapped Mrs. Mayfield. "Come into the house."

"In a moment, Mama. Jem?"

"Excuse me, miss. I just need to rest a minute."

"You are worn out, poor boy. How long have you been on the road?"

"Four days."

She surveyed his white face and shaking hands. "When did you eat last?"

Jem looked down. "I used all the money yesterday, and—"

"Come along," interrupted Margaret firmly. "We will

go to the kitchens first, and then you shall tell me what has happened."

Mrs. Mayfield called again, but Margaret ignored her.

Settled with a large slice of cold meat pie, Jem was much better, and he had soon told Margaret his story. She was on her feet and pacing before he was done, her heart flaming with eagerness and hope. "Of course we will go at once," she said. "Or—can you ride, Jem?"

"Course I can. I was just hungry." He finished the pie in one huge bite and mumbled through it, "I'm ready."

Margaret laughed. "You have a little time. I must pack some things. You can have another slice."

Jem gazed at the remaining pie avidly.

"Go on. I'll come back when I'm ready." She left him cutting another portion and went into the front hall. As she put her foot on the bottom step, however, her mother emerged from the library.

"Margaret, come in here," she said. "We want to speak to you."

"I'm sorry, Mama, but I'm in a great hurry. There's been an accident, and I must go back to Cornwall at once."

"Out of the question." Mrs. Mayfield folded her arms and glared.

Margaret hesitated. She could pretend to be cowed and then slip away as she had done the last time. This might be easier than arguing with her parents. But she did not want to. She was capable of making her own decisions, and it was time they realized this. Without speaking, she walked into the library, her mother just behind. Her father was standing behind his desk. "So, what is all this?" he said when she came in.

"There has been an accident, Papa, and I must go back to Cornwall."

"Nonsense. I forbid it, of course. An accident to whom?"

"Sir Justin."

"*Hah*. A transparent attempt to lure you back into his clutches."

"Oh, Papa."

"Whatever it is, you certainly cannot go," put in Mrs. Mayfield. "I cannot believe that you would entertain the idea for a moment. Indeed, Margaret, you are dreadfully changed. First at the party and now *this*." She almost shuddered.

"Yes, I *am* changed. And because I am, there is nothing you can do to stop me from leaving."

Her parents drew themselves up.

"Even if you lock me in my room, I shall climb out the window and go."

"*Margaret*," exclaimed both at once.

"So, you see, you had best let me do what I think right."

"Right?" Her mother was rigid with astonishment and outrage.

"I will be going as soon as I pack a few things," finished the girl, and she turned on her heel and left the room, her parents gaping after her.

In less than half an hour she was ready. She wore her riding habit and had hurriedly thrust some things into a bandbox. She felt queer. This was so like, and yet so unlike, her previous journey. She fetched Jem from the kitchen and ordered their horses, but the footman to whom she spoke shuffled nervously and did not reply. Suspecting that her parents had told the servants not to obey her, she gave Jem the bandbox and led the way to the stables, where together they saddled their mounts under the scandalized and disapproving eye of the head groom. It was not until they were starting down the avenue before the house that Margaret saw her parents again. They stood together on the front steps, looking angry and somehow bewildered. "If you go," said her mother, "we positively disown you. You needn't come back."

These words hurt, and Margaret experienced a moment of doubt, as if she had been struck a sudden sharp blow and could not at once recover all her wits. But then she straightened and nodded, turning her horse's head away.

"*Margaret,*" cried her father, anguish in his voice.

"I'm sorry," she replied, and, with a signal to Jem, urged her horse to a brisker pace.

The journey that followed was never very clear to Margaret afterward. She rode doggedly, her mind too full for talk or observation. She let Jem find their road, and she did not even notice when the sun began to descend and the air cooled. It was nearly dark before the boy pulled up and indicated that they were approaching the village. "It ain't nearly as far as I thought," he added. "I was all over the countryside trying to find where you had gone. I must have rode four times the distance."

"How much farther?" asked Margaret, looking around for a landmark in the gathering dusk.

"Only 'bout a mile."

"Let us go on, then."

In a short while they were riding along the lane toward the Red Lion. The windows were lit, and Margaret strained to see a familiar figure, but no one appeared. Jem took charge of her horse when she slid off, and she hurried into the inn, only to nearly collide with Mrs. Appleby, who was starting up the stairs with a heavy tray. "*Miss,*" cried the latter. "You have come, then."

"As soon as Jem found me. Why did you not write?"

The landlady again told the story of the papers.

"Papa. How could he?"

"Where is that barley water?" called Mrs. Dowling from above.

"Coming," replied Mrs. Appleby, moving again.

Margaret followed her. "How is he? Jem said he had a fever."

"He has that. Carrie Dowling says he's better, but I must say I can't see it myself. His head is that hot."

"Did he ask for me?"

"He can't *ask* for no one, miss. He isn't talking sense. But he does call out your name."

Margaret took a deep breath. They reached the upper floor, and Mrs. Dowling came out of Keighley's bedchamber to meet them. "So, you're here," she said to Margaret.

"I came at once."

The old woman nodded. "You'll do him good."

Margaret had never heard pleasanter words. She felt suffused with a warmth that threatened to bubble over in highly inappropriate laughter.

"Let me have that barley water," continued Mrs. Dowling. "He's fair parched."

They went into the room. Keighley lay on his back, breathing harshly. Margaret went over to him and put out a hand to brush back his dark hair. He was terribly pale, and his nostrils had a pinched look. Now and then he murmured a broken phrase too soft to understand. "How is he, really?" Margaret whispered.

"He's bad," replied Mrs. Dowling. "He pulled that shoulder out, and then he was lying in the storm for a day and a night."

"Will he be all right?"

"I hope so, miss. You can help him, I think."

"I will do *anything*. I can nurse him."

"It's not so much that. He calls for you, you see."

Margaret smiled tremulously.

"And I thought that if you were here to answer him, he might rest easier. He thrashes around so sometimes that I worry his shoulder will never heal."

"I will do whatever you say."

Mrs. Dowling nodded, smiling slightly. "Well, just

now you can sit down over there. You'll see what I mean when he speaks."

She did as she was told, but for two hours nothing happened except that Mrs. Dowling changed the compresses on Keighley's forehead and tried to get him to swallow barley water. Then, as eleven o'clock approached, their patient became restless. His head rolled back and forth on the pillow, and his inarticulate muttering got louder.

"There he goes," said Mrs. Dowling. "You come and talk to him, miss. See if you can calm him."

Margaret bent over the bed. "Sir Justin," she said softly. "Justin?"

Her voice seemed to have no effect, and he continued to shift uneasily. Then, without warning, he stiffened and cried, *"Margaret. No."*

The girl did not need Mrs. Dowling's signal. She bent closer and said, "It's all right. Everything is all right. I'm here."

There was an instant's silence, then to her amazement, Keighley opened his eyes and gazed into hers. "Margaret?"

She took his hand, which lay limply on the counterpane. "Yes. I'm here. Everything is all right."

"Mistake," murmured Keighley weakly.

"Don't worry. You must think only of getting well."

"Don't leave," he gasped out.

"I shan't. I shall stay right here until you are better."

He smiled shakily, then lapsed into unconsciousness once more.

21

After that night, though Keighley remained unconscious, his recovery began. His breathing became less labored toward dawn, and Mrs. Dowling was able to get a good bit of liquid into him. The following afternoon, he broke out in a profuse sweat and then fell into a more natural sleep, a development that led his nurse to pronounce him out of danger. "He'll be weak," she warned Margaret. "It'll be a good while before he's on his feet again. But the worst is over."

"Thank God." Margaret leaned back in the armchair with a great sigh.

"I'm going home for a spell. Annie's here to watch him. You should rest."

"I don't want to leave him. He might wake again."

"If he does, you'll be told. You don't want him to wake to find you collapsed on his floor, do you? You haven't slept at all."

Margaret smiled. "Well, perhaps I'll go outside. I could use some air."

Mrs. Dowling shrugged. "You'd do better to go to bed," she replied as she went out.

Sleep was clearly out of the question. Margaret stood gazing down at Keighley as Annie Appleby slipped into the room. She could not sleep while he lay so still and silent. But she was stiff and tired. A short walk might revive her enough to stay beside him through another night. So, telling Annie she would be back soon, she went downstairs and out into the street.

The late August day was surprisingly cool, the sky overcast, and the wind fresh. But she decided not to go back for a shawl. She walked down to the seawall and gazed out over the gray waves, each tipped with a fleck of foam. Then, the wind picking at her skirts, she went along to the steps and down to her secret pool. It was just the same, deeply quiet and serene. Margaret felt tears in her eyes as she stood there looking down. The days she had been away were erased. Here time did not seem to intrude or to matter.

She stayed longer than she had meant to, and when she returned to the Red Lion, she was told that Keighley had wakened briefly in her absence and asked for her. "I told him you were out walking, miss," said Annie. "And he smiled a little and went back to sleep."

Margaret bowed her head, bitterly disappointed, and vowed not to leave Keighley's bedside until she had spoken to him again. She sent Annie down to get her dinner and settled in the armchair with a book. The evening slowly passed. Mrs. Dowling looked in, pronounced Keighley improving still, and left again. Margaret began to feel drowsy and put her book aside. She had not slept for two days, and only her concern for Sir Justin kept her awake now.

As midnight came and went she continued to nod, and at last her head sank back on the chair and she slept.

The inn was silent except for the customary creakings of an old building. A mouse scratched in the wainscoting along the stairs, and the parlor clock ticked more loudly than it dared during the day. At two in the morning Sir Justin suddenly opened his eyes and looked around with perfect lucidity. He gazed at his bedchamber, at the guttering candle on the table beside him, and then saw Margaret peacefully curled in the armchair, breathing quietly.

Keighley smiled. Seeing her like this, unaware and defenseless, made something tighten in the region of his heart. If he had not been sure before, he would now have known that he loved her. The feeling was so pervasive and wonderful that he did not even regret his foolish behavior any longer. That was past; everything would come right.

As if sensing his thoughts, Margaret woke. She blinked twice and then sat up, shaking out her crumpled dress and taking a deep breath. Only then did she become aware of his regard. "Oh! You're awake."

"Yes."

She rose and went to stand beside him. "How do you feel?"

"Perfectly normal. Weak."

"You strained your wound badly. And caught a fever."

"It was no more than I deserved, for behaving like an idiot."

Margaret's eyes widened as she gazed into his.

"I must apologize to you," he added.

"Oh, no."

"Indeed, yes. I treated you shockingly." He looked around. "Is your father still here?"

"No, he is at home."

"He left you alone? I cannot believe it."

"N-No. I . . . I have been home as well. When you disappeared, you see . . ."

He nodded grimly.

"Then, when you were found, Jem came to fetch me."

"And you simply returned."

"Of course."

He gazed at her. "Your parents did not object?"

She grimaced. "Well, yes. But I told them I had to come. And they were angry with me in any case because of the party."

"The party?" he repeated bemusedly.

"The squire's luncheon. I told Mr. Twitchel that the laboring men should have the vote."

"You . . ." He laughed weakly. "You did *not*, Margaret."

"Oh, yes, and a great many other things. I have never seen our neighbors so shocked."

"I can imagine it. But I wish I had seen it."

"Yes. So, since I have become a radical, my parents will probably be glad to be rid of me."

"I doubt it." He watched her. "A radical. I really have ruined you, haven't I, Margaret?"

She stiffened. *"No."*

"But I have. You are alienated from your parents and friends. And your stay in this inn has finally and certainly compromised you. I have much to apologize for."

"Don't be silly. I should much rather know the truth than have Mr. Twitchel as a friend. And my parents—"

"Yes?"

"Well, they will get over the shock, and I daresay we shall patch it up."

"I hope so."

Margaret stared at him. Was he about to tell her that she should go home to her parents?

"I shouldn't like you to go through life battling your family."

She kept her eyes on his.

"It would be a sad thing for our children to see."

"Our . . ."

Keighley slowly lifted his hand and put it over hers. "I am in poor shape for lovemaking. Will you marry me, Margaret?"

Her blue eyes lit, but she said, "Are you sure you wish me to? You said you did not."

"At last, yes, I am sure. I took a damnably long time to know my own mind, and I behaved like a fool because of it. But now I *am* certain."

Margaret sank down on the bed and held his hand tightly. "In that case I should be delighted to marry you."

He smiled and tried to raise his head. "Curse this weakness. I can't even kiss you. Come here."

She bent down to him, and he managed to get one arm round her. They kissed passionately till Margaret once again felt that melting sensation she had discovered earlier in his arms. She moved closer, half lying on the bed next to him. Their lips separated, then drew irresistibly together again. When this long kiss ended, Keighley laughed a little. "Perhaps it's a lucky thing I am weak," he said. "I couldn't answer for my self-control in this situation if I were not."

Suddenly realizing her scandalous posture, Margaret started to draw away.

"Oh, no, my dear. As your father so presciently put it, I have you in my power now." He grinned maniacally, and Margaret laughed. "I shan't let you go until you kiss me again."

"Tyrant," murmured Margaret, leaning against him.

"In this, always."

"And what, sir, has become of your radical principles?"

He raised one brow. "Alas, they are apparently not so firmly entrenched as I believed."

"*Justin.*"

"You must help me bear my lapse," he added, drawing her close along the length of his body.

It was some time before they spoke again, but then Margaret sat up. "Annie might come in," she protested.

"The Applebys are thoroughly shocked by us already," he retorted, but he let her move away. "Shall we be married here to reassure them?"

"Oh, I should like that." Margaret thought a moment. "But Mama—"

"Will wish to exhibit us to all and sundry."

"Do you mind too much?" wondered the girl. "About everything, I mean. My family and—"

"I would endure much more to have you," he answered. "Though when I think of binding your father to my mother, my blood does run cold, I admit."

She smiled. "They will have a great deal in common. They can talk politics."

"*Talk*. Well, we must just make certain that any weapons are removed from the vicinity beforehand."

Margaret laughed.

"But that problem may be left for later. Now everything is perfect." He extended his hand invitingly.

"Except Jem. You must buy him a new boat, you know."

He groaned. "I destroyed the *Gull*, didn't I?"

"Utterly."

"Well, I will buy him one. Or anything else he likes. Without him I never would have discovered my sweet, radical love."

There was, of course, only one answer to this, and, throwing caution to the winds, Margaret gladly gave it.

About the Author

Jane Ashford grew up in the American Midwest. A lifelong love of English literature led her eventually to a doctorate in English and to extensive travel in England. After working as a teacher and an editor, she began to write, drawing on her knowledge of eighteenth- and nineteenth-century history. She is a determined fair-weather sailor. She now divides her time between New York City and Lakeville, Connecticut.